More, More, More!

Published by Phaze Books

PHAZE
Cincinnati, Ohio

www.Phaze.com

More, More, More!

a collection of big, beautiful erotic romance by

SAMMIE JO MORESCA
MEG WINSTON
LEIGH ELLWOOD
VICTORIA BLISSE

Cincinnati, Ohio

A Phaze Production
Phaze Books
6470A Glenway Avenue, #109
Cincinnati, OH 45211-5222
Phaze is an imprint of Mundania Press, LLC.

To order additional copies of this book, contact:
books@phaze.com
www.Phaze.com

Cover art © 2008 Debi Lewis
Edited by Denise Jeffries, Kathryn Lively, and Kent Miller

Trade Paperback ISBN-13: 978-1-60659-057-7

First Print Edition - September, 2008
Printed in the United States of America

10 9 8 7 6 5 4 3 2 1

Table of Contents

Diet Another Day
Sammie Jo Moresca

Also by Sammie Jo Moresca

Smolder
Type Dirty to Me
Son of a Preacher Man

Fontainebleau Resort and Spa, Miami Beach, Florida

"Remember, this is a team effort. Your roommate will be your lifeline when the chocolate calls. Don't let her fail you. The team that loses the most on the Body Mass Index at the end of the month will be awarded the spokesperson's contract worth upwards of forty thousand dollars," said the trim boot camp diva of ceremonies with legs of steel. She had her audience riveted.

Crystal couldn't have cared less about becoming an infomercial diva. She wanted a new life. As she looked around at controlled applause in the sea of pink skirt suits in subtle shades from cloud to fuchsia, she finger-combed her long, mousy brown hair and squirmed, tugging on her size 1X stretch jeans, to make her thighs and crotch comfortable. Giving up, she flicked a tiny dandruff flake off her black ribbed tank top and tucked her errant white bra strap back underneath.

One other soul stood out. Seated in the rigid conference chair next to her was her Scottish e-pal Rosaleen Dalrymple, who'd talked her into this retreat. Bespectacled, frizzy redheaded Rosaleen wore an ankle length, blue plaid jumper, dingy grey tee shirt with armpit stains, and plastic flip flops. Crystal shook her head. Had she any idea how Roslaeen dressed, perhaps she would have treated her to a new outfit or two.

"As you'll see on page forty-one, along with a strict ten carbohydrates per day diet, the exercise component is straightforward. Activity, ladies. The best and safest way for you *Sofa Sherries* to begin is walking. The valet will not release your Mercedes until after graduation. Cabs will not carry you, the buses will not shuttle. Don't even think of renting one of those cute little motorized scooters you see models zipping around on. Use your large muscles, ladies. Build endurance. Increase your aerobic capacity."

The women applauded again.

Crystal was on board. *Yes. I can walk. Yes, if my meals are prepared, I can adjust to a restricted carbohydrate diet. All of the support will be fun. Just like college. Or what my impression of college is like from books.* A wave of shame tried to overtake Crystal. *Everybody here probably has at least a bachelor's degree. And a fabulous career.*

"You will be assigned a canteen. Keep it filled and with you at all times. Optimum water intake is twelve eight-ounce servings per day. Strive to hit that target exactly. No more, no less. And subsequently, ladies, you need to feel free to pee. With two hundred women on the same schedule, the designated restrooms at this conference center will prove inadequate. Do not waste time in line. Guard the door of the men's room and take turns. A body waiting in line for a toilet is not a body in motion burning fat. If you stand in line for five minutes every time nature calls this month, you will be two pounds heavier. It's not worth it, ladies."

Uproarious laughter and nods filled the room.

No wonder I'm fat. Wow. I had no idea. Yes, absolutely I'll use the men's room. All right then, two pounds guaranteed weight loss. Check.

"Turn to page forty-eight. Tomorrow's itinerary: Breakfast in the Palm ballroom from five-fifteen to five thirty-five. Feel free to mingle and meet the other ladies. Most of you are sales consultants with the Patty Unger Cosmetics Company. Enjoy chatting with your counterparts from other states and territories. After breakfast, you all have a rigid list of activities to achieve before lunch at high noon, back in the Palm ballroom. You and your roommate are responsible for each other's successful completion. Don't be a weak link."

The ladies applauded yet again. Crystal turned to Rosaleen. The friends smiled and nodded in unison.

Crystal skimmed the activities. This sounded fun. A sunrise stretching period on the beach. Power walking in the saltwater pool. A four-minute restroom break. Thirty-six minutes on the cardio machines. Sweat a few pounds off in the sauna. Power Pilates. Thirty minutes to shower and dress for lunch.

"Our afternoons are for spiritual growth. We will meet for a prayer session on the beach, in front of the first lifeguard stand to the left of the steps. We will rotate through the world's religions. Deeply contemplate the messages. Open your heart to your maker. Accept Him in different forms through the hearts of your peers."

Yeah, yeah, yeah, whatever. At least we'll get to relax.

"At one PM, you will break off into groups for barefoot beach walking. Please arrive in a suitable bathing suit with ample sunscreen, SPF fifty or higher, sunglasses, and sun bonnets. Each group will receive a unique novel to read while walking. Yes, ladies. We will learn to integrate exercise seamlessly into our lives. You can, and will, walk and read a book. Be prepared for a pop quiz at breakfast each morning, on the previous day's book."

Is she kidding? I'm supposed to read and walk and finish the book in one day? And not collapse of heat exhaustion? Miami in July. What was I thinking, signing on for this? Crystal's enthusiasm took a sudden nose dive which she felt in the pit of her growling stomach. She turned to Rosaleen, who had an alarmed expression on her blotchy face.

The boot camp commander continued, "For our first week's reward, we have arranged to have a mixer with the Homeland Security First Responders Conference. Cocktail dresses are required. Don't forget hose, a minimum three-inch heel, and full make up."

Cocktail dress? Sausage casings and lip balm? Great. Homeland Security First Responders? Oh, don't they sound like a fun bunch? Crystal envisioned a group of fat, balding fifty-somethings so uptight they dance you suspiciously through metal detectors.

"All right, ladies. Retrieve your luggage from the holding area. Please form a line, two across with your roommate. Heads up, breasts high. Walk proudly through the hotel and out into the night to our dormitories at the Jesuit school."

Dormitories? Jesuit school? "Rosaleen, what's she talking about? I thought we were booked here at the hotel."

"Only for the meetings, meals, and spa services. We are rooming in the dorms to keep us away from temptation."

"In other words, they want to keep us from ordering room service."

"Exactly."

Two by two, they waddled through the automatic revolving door and into the night. Stars glistened on the surface of the Intracoastal Waterway. A cruise boat was docked. *If we get any downtime, maybe Rosaleen and I can take a tour.* They marched on the sidewalk, clip clopping and huffing.

As the wind gusted through the coco palm-lined avenue, Crystal pulled hair out of her mouth. She could make out the pink sensible heels of the women directly in front of her, so she didn't part her hair often. When they stopped at the light at the causeway, Crystal looked in awe at how no one else's hair was moving. *They must use Patty Unger's helmet hairspray.* She grinned. Crystal preferred purchasing her cosmetics and hair care products at the local discount store for pennies on the dollar. It occurred to her the great irony in Rosaleen. She was gung ho to compete in a Patty Unger Cosmetics sponsored contest, yet she took no care in her appearance.

As they marched across Collins Avenue, she wondered just how far the Jesuit school was. Her stomach flip-flopped as she switched hands holding her suitcase, and shoved Rosaleen to the outside. The bridge swayed beneath their feet and convertibles whizzed by, all with radios set to different stations. The horn o'plenty grated in her head. *Cruella de Vil did say something about no caffeine, didn't she? Just great. I'm already in withdrawal and I hadn't even been deprived yet.*

Finally, around a dimly lit corner, the ladies snaked onto a concrete path through a black wrought iron gate. A Spanish style, four-story building loomed. As Crystal wrestled her suitcase up the steps and over the metal threshold, her eyes settled on the torn green felt of a pool table and a large sofa clad in a faded orange floral slipcover.

A woman with a clipboard read her badge. "Levitan?"

Crystal nodded.

She looked at Rosaleen. "Dalrymple?"

"Aye." She sniffed.

"Room four twenty-three. Here are your codes. If you lose them, your house mother is in room four oh two. She has a copy, and also the first aid kit. Be sure to find her room, so you can locate her quickly when you need treatments for blisters and heat exhaustion." She handed them each a small slip of paper with *Room 423* and *Code 0901* typed.

The elevator line was more of a mosh pit. Crystal followed Rosaleen up three double flights of stairs, nervous that her mammoth hiking backpack would crush her if she toppled backwards.

"Four oh two. This is the house mother's room."

"Aye," Rosaleen lamented.

They wove through the musty labyrinth to the end of the hall. A window overlooked a mystery. Crystal couldn't tell what because a banana tree fully blocked the view. Rosaleen adjusted her black, plastic Harry Potter glasses and keyed in the code. She pushed the door open and fumbled for the light switch. Crystal followed her in.

"Right or left?" Rosaleen asked.

Crystal peered around her. A closet, twin bed, and desk lined each wall. "Doesn't matter."

Rosaleen wrestled with her backpack. Crystal assisted her as Rosaleen lowered it onto the right bunk and commenced crying.

"What's wrong? Did I catch your skin in the backpack? I'm so sorry."

"No. It's Dickie."

Here we go with the Dickie business again. Crystal flipped on the bathroom light. There was an old shower stall, toilet, and door to the next room. The sink and mirror were by the hall door in the bedroom. At least they wouldn't have to wait for the Patty Unger ladies to paint their faces. Crystal used the facility, then unpacked.

Rosaleen curled in a ball, sobbing. Crystal offered her a box of Kleenex. She accepted and blew. And blew and blew.

"Can I get you anything?"

"No."

"Do you want to talk?"

"No."

She was guiltily relieved. It wasn't like Rosaleen hadn't been complaining about Dickie online for three years, and Crystal never did figure out what the rift was.

A sweet southern voice called out, "Knock, knock, knock! You hoo! It's your suite neighbors, may we come in?" Two painted ladies burst into Crystal and Rosaleen's room through the shared bathroom.

The bubbly woman in her twenties reminded Crystal of a plus-size model on the QVC home shopping channel. She said her name was Tiffany. The sour puss behind her reminded Crystal of a hippopotamus in pink stilettos who really needed to get back underwater. Her name was Hilda.

Rosaleen blew her nose and extended her hand. Tiffany stepped over to the bunk and shook it. "I'm Rosaleen..." she gestured toward Crystal, "and this is my best mate in the whole world, Crystal."

Crystal smiled and shook hands with Tiffany. Hilda just stood with her hands on her hippo hips and glared at Crystal. A shudder went through her. Memories of a junior high school bully festered open.

When the introductions were over and the neighbors stepped back into their room, Crystal closed and locked the bathroom door leading into her and Rosaleen's room. "How dare they just barge right in here!"

Rosaleen said, "Tiffany seemed sweet but the big troll...how rude. Let's be sure to keep our door locked."

The girls brushed and flossed and changed into cotton nightgowns. At exactly ten o'clock, the building went dark. The mattress was firm, but the pillow seemed like a lumpy bowl of oatmeal. Thunder crashed as lightening flashed shadows in through the window.

Later, Crystal lay on the edge of her bed with one leg dangling over the side. Not by choice, but water was dripping through the moldy ceiling tiles in every other location in the room, so Rosaleen was now sharing her bunk.

In between crying fits, Rosaleen snored like a lioness. She'd elbowed Crystal twice in the neck as she lay staring at the red LED numbers on the alarm clock. At four thirty-three, Crystal had yet to doze off. She jumped up screaming when Rosaleen sliced her leg with a toenail.

* * * *

They survived the first day of boot camp. After a delicious dinner of parsley and kohlrabi slathered in mayonnaise, Crystal walked stiffly toward the ladies room. The aroma of pizza from the Panther ballroom caused her to stop at the door, close her eyes, and inhale. Oh, did she want just one slice. Just one whole pie. Just one cheesecake.

Hearing the approach of voices, Crystal opened her eyes, smoothed her wrinkled yellow cotton capris, and smiled at the two men leaving the room. They looked right through her.

Just wait. By the end of the month, I'll be fifty pounds lighter with long, lean muscles, pert breasts and behind, no cellulite or wrinkles. Well, maybe I'll be ten pounds lighter, and maybe my panties will fully cover my behind again.

The last man from the room emerged, his eyes wild as he pointed to his throat.

The universal sign of choking. Crystal asked, "Can you speak?"

He shook his head.

Crystal spun him around and hugged him from behind. Making one hand into a fist with the other

16

clamped over it, she positioned it in the space between his ribs and sternum. By the second inward and upward thrust, he was spitting a long string of mozzarella cheese onto the floor. One last thrust and he said, "Thank you."

"Did I hurt you?"

"No."

Crystal stepped around the cheese and grabbed a hunk of napkins from the table just inside the ballroom. As she cleaned, a shudder overtook her.

"You could have died!" she said, tears dripping down her cheeks. She threw the mess in a trash can.

"I'm prepared to die. Every day on duty, I know it might be my last shift. But I am not ready to let a pizza be my grim reaper."

Crystal didn't know whether to laugh or not.

He grabbed her hand and said, "I'm Spenser Edwards."

He had a firm grip and Crystal immediately noticed his long fingers. Her thoughts turned to what they say about men with long fingers. She demurely looked him up and down. He was a good six inches taller. Khaki naval work uniform. A sailor. He smiled when she finally looked at his chiseled face. Clean shaven, long lashes framed sparkling brown eyes. Brown hair immaculately cut into a very short flat top.

Crystal realized he was still holding her hand. Her gaze shifted to his left hand. No ring. No tell-tale tan line. "I need to get going."

"Can't I buy you a drink or something?"

Oh yeah. I'll have a cosmopolitan, and you can dribble it over me naked. "No, I have to get back." She headed out the door. "It was nice meeting you."

"Wait. What's your name?"

"Crystal. Crystal Bee Levitan."

She hurried back to the conference room, worried she'd be scolded for being AWOL. She slipped in a side door just before the team leader dismissed them for the day.

The sailor was waiting for her when she emerged. "Hello, Crystal."

To say her heart went pitter-patter was right on target.

"Rosaleen, go on ahead. I'll catch up."

* * * *

The whirlpool pummeling her lower back was a welcome hurt-so-good kind of pain to her exercise abused body. Crystal was sore in places she didn't know contained muscles. Her tendons hurt. Her ligaments hurt. Her veins hurt. And she couldn't believe she was in this five-hundred-dollar a night suite, sipping a room service cosmopolitan in a sailor's candlelit bathroom. Well, do a good deed and you get rewarded sometimes. It was very kind of him to let her have an evening respite from the grueling boot camp. She certainly didn't want to be stuck in the dorm room listening to Rosaleen sobbing and slinging snot.

Crystal tipped the martini glass and tickled the last pink drop with her tongue. It had been lovely taking a walk on the rich side of the tracks, but she needed to get back to the dormitory and try to sleep. Stepping out of the tub onto the plush white bathmat, she wrapped a humongous bath sheet around her and toweled off. A candlelit reflection in the wall mirror caught her breath. She couldn't be the alluring woman staring back. It must be the booze on a nearly starved stomach. Maybe she could hint for the officer and a gentleman to order just one more round before she left.

Perhaps he might even be inclined to intoxicate her in the way only a man can do. Slipping into the red hotel robe, Crystal left it loosely tied, so some cleavage would show. All men loved large breasts.

He was seated fireside, sipping from a fluted crystal glass. An ice bucket with a magnum of champagne chilled next to a bouquet of pink roses. Her gaze watched his eyes, hooded with seduction. She walked over to him and licked the rim of his glass. *Oh, my gosh. I didn't just do that.*

"This is your night, Crystal." He tilted the glass and poured it into her mouth. She swallowed the sweet bubbles. They popped as he refilled it. She felt his eyes on the creamy flesh peeking from her crimson robe.

She seized the glass and downed it with one gulp. He took it back from her and placed it on the mantle. Removing the frosty bottle, he took her hand and walked toward the French doors. Opening one enough to allow her admittance to the bedroom, she abruptly stopped at the site of the king-sized bed. In the moonlight from the open drapery, and from the two flickering candles on the nightstands, the headboard looked to be about eight feet tall and ornately engraved. A white gossamer canopy billowed down from a cathedral ceiling. She heard

Spenser close the door as her eyes adjusted to the naked man on the bed. Her breath hitched. Spenser said, "Crystal, I'd like you to meet Tim."

"It's wonderful to meet you, Crystal." He reached for her.

Both men waited for her response.

"What's going on here?" she demurely asked, knowing she must be dreaming, or hallucinating from dehydration.

Tim replied, "We're here to pleasure you, Crystal."

"Both of you?"

Spenser huskily replied, "Yes."

"No. Absolutely not." *What kind of sick trap have I fallen into? I should have known better than to have come to a stranger's room.*

Spenser undressed and slid onto the bed next to Tim. They both looked expectantly at Crystal. Tim asked, "Won't you please join us?"

She ran back to the bathroom and scooped up her clothes. Spenser followed her. "What's wrong? I'm so sorry, we didn't mean to frighten you."

"I should have never come here. Thanks for the bath and drinks, but I'm not who you think I am."

"What do you mean?"

A tear trickled down her face as she slipped on one shoe. He caught it on his fingertip.

"Oh, no, Crystal. Don't cry. We didn't mean to make you cry. What's wrong?"

"You two are gay and have a bet going to see if one of you can do a fat girl."

Tim joined them. "We are not gay and there is no bet. But you are right about one thing."

"We prefer beautiful, full figured women."

They each took one of her hands and led her back into the bedroom.

Spenser said, "You are the most desirable woman I've ever laid eyes on.

With that, she took a big pull straight from the champagne bottle and let the robe puddle onto the floor. She nervously lay down on the bed nearest Tim. She shivered as he ran a finger across her cheek. The breeze from the ocean rustled the sheer curtains.

Wiggling into the cool, white satin sheets, Crystal closed her eyes and inhaled the moment. Fingers massaged her scalp and she sighed. Fingers brushed the bottoms of her feet and she giggled, opening her eyes and squirming away onto the floor.

Tim leaned down and grabbed her arm. "Are you all right?"

"Yes. This is just so silly." *What am I doing? Please don't let anything heinous happen to me tonight.*

Crystal you worry too much. For once in your life, let yourself go. Carpe Diem. So what if they're serial killers. At least they're cute. And how long has it been since I've even been asked on a real date? Oh...yeah, right. Never have been. The guys all just want to be friends that have sex then pretend they never did it with me

But these men want me. In this ritzy hotel room in paradise. I'm going to set my inhibitions aside and let nature take its lovely course this time. For once I feel desired.

Tim eyed Spenser.

Crystal stood up as soon as she realized she was naked on the hotel carpet. She nearly blacked out, but her equilibrium righted itself in time.

Spenser offered, "We're here to pleasure you. Let us know what your tiniest wish is and we'll launch you to the stars."

Crystal was glad the clouds had so expediently moved in front of the moon and the room had darkened considerably. She hoped they couldn't see her withholding another giggle in the candlelight.

She sat on the bed, and scooted in between the two men.

"Guys, I'm a plain vanilla girl. As far as erotic delights, I enjoy one man, a little foreplay, missionary sex, then a great afterglow nap."

Spenser said, "But you deserve so much more. You can have double your pleasure. He plumped her breast and gently kissed the nipple. Tim lowered his lips on its twin. She lay back and smiled as they suckled. Maybe they were onto something. Someone's hand slipped down to her curly hair as she sat up, pulling away.

"I'm sorry, fellas, but I'm just not the *ménage a trois* kinda girl."

Spenser said, "Relax, we'll show you how."

"I hardly know you and I've never even seen him with his clothes on. How do you guys know each other? What is your last name, Tim? And what do you do for a living?"

"Tim and I were in the Air Force together. Stationed at the base of a glacier in Alaska."

"I'm a personal trainer now," said Tim.

I'm no fool. I know that was a Navy uniform Spenser had on. What's their game? Crystal's mind wandered to cheesecake. Real yummy cheesecake with a graham cracker crust and cherries on top. With a side of chocolate chip ice cream. "Can we order dessert?"

Tim reached for the phone. "Sure. What would you like?"

"Tell them to send up one of each."

He did.

"So what did you guys do on the glacier?" *I'll play along with this delicious charade.* She tried to listen as Spenser spewed forth military lingo and Tim interjected memorable incidents of helicopters missing the landing sites.

"So what did you guys do on your down time, in between heroic adventures?"

Spenser said, "Watched porn videos."

Tim seemed to grin.

"And waited for female airmen to fly in and console your neglected members?"

"No female pilots on that mission."

"So, you guys are gay. That explains a lot. I'm here because of some sort of bet." Her stomach knotted as she tried to scramble away.

Tim pulled her back and said, "No. Not at all. We love breasts and vaginas."

My, isn't he formal. "So you guys watched close ups of women doing men and other women, and then what?"

"We jerked off. What else?" Spenser replied. "Why, what do you imagine we did?"

A knock on the door sent Spenser to answer, wrapping the bedspread around him as he left.

Tim kissed her. Not a gentle friendly kiss, but full-on explosive tongue action. This talk was evidently turning him on. He moaned as both hands worked her breasts, kneading them and rubbing the nipples roughly with his thumbs.

Oh, yeah. This was just the kind of lovemaking Crystal liked. But wait, he was kissing her other lips, too. But how could that be? She reached her hand down and felt Spenser's hair. She tried to pull away and sit up, but the men held their ground. Held her down. Tim took both of her wrists in one hand and held them over her head as he kissed her deeper. She alternated concentrating on her mouth and her writhing lower half. Too many sensations. Delicious sensations.

As Spenser flicked his tongue, serpent like, down below, she was embarrassed to smell her juices. Tim pulled both nipples into one hand and rubbed them vigorously as he continued to devour her mouth. Once Spenser switched from flicking to sucking, she knew the point of no return had arrived. Squeezing his head between her thighs, she bucked as she rode her wave to nirvana.

Tim pulled away to hear the scream as he suckled and lightly bit a nipple.

Crystal opened her eyes and wiggled away from them. The clouds had passed by the moon, for she could see her lovers. Gods. "I may be dreaming, but don't wake me yet."

Tim said, "We won't wake you, baby. We're going to rock you all night long."

He looked a lot like Spenser, only a little younger. Same military doo and coloring. Nice cleft chin. Cary Grant-ish. Her eyes dropped across his broad shoulders. She lightly touched his bare chest and ran her hands down his six-pack, stopping just above his erection. Gazing over at Spenser, he too stood at attention. She looked back and forth, marveling at the comparison. Tim was longer and straighter with his vein throbbing on top. Spenser was an inch shy, but he made up for it in girth.

She closed her legs as she sat up. "The ice cream is melting."

Tim fetched a banana split with a crisp biscotti garnish. He handed it to her and she dove in. Between bites she asked, "So tell me what you'd do when you'd watch those girls with the implants do lesi things to each other. You guys like watching that, don't you?"

Spenser said, "Yeah, of course. It's only natural."

"And you jerked off in front of each other?"

Tim said, "Kinda."

"Kinda what?"

"Maybe we might have helped each other a time or two."

"I knew it! All guys have low morals and will hump anything."

Spenser insisted, "We aren't gay. So maybe we touched each other's tools a little, but there was never any..."

Crystal pulled a long banana half out of the glass bowl and licked it from tip to tip. "Show me what you guys did."

* * * *

Spenser's hopes plummeted. *Great. Busted. Caught. Need to come up with a plausible way to get out of this. She knows we've never done this sort of thing before.* He looked over at Tim, who had retrieved the magnum of champagne and was propped up on pillows next to Crystal. He wouldn't meet Spenser's eyes.

"All right. So we didn't watch porn videos and jerk off."

Crystal giggled. "So you guys are just as vanilla as me. Touché."

Tim swallowed a big gulp and drizzled one drop onto Crystal's arm. He licked it and said, "So we're inexperienced in menages. But you've got to admit, darling, we're pretty quick studies."

"So were you even in the Air Force at all?"

Tim replied, "Navy."

Spenser added, "Yes, we really did spend a tour of duty at the base of a glacier. We're physicians. Treated a lot of frostbite."

Crystal set the bowl of ice cream on a nightstand. Spenser carried it out to the living room, placed it on the cart, and detoured to the bathroom. He returned to find Tim taking Crystal's pulse.

"What are you doing?"

Crystal said, "Playing doctor. *If* you guys really are doctors, no sense in passing up a free check-up."

"I'm glad we've got that out in the open."

"Hunh?" Crystal giggled as Tim placed two fingers on the artery inside her thigh.

Spenser said, "We're researching weight loss."

"So you just happened to choke on pizza in front of a fat girl, to lure her into your boudoir to get an up close, inside out view of her fat?"

Tim snorted. "And what a pleasurable consultation. But no, darling, we're here for the Homeland Security First Responders conference. Serendipity brought you and Spenser together."

Crystal stood up and headed for the bathroom. When she closed the door, Spenser sat on the bed next to Tim.

Tim whispered, "She's a whole lotta woman. Much more than a mouthful, better than those saline girls. I can't wait to pump into her cleavage."

"The goal isn't for us to get off here. Focus on the control study. *Her orgasms* are key."

"Your cock's been just as rigid as mine, pal. You can't tell me it's all about the mission."

"Sure it is. Whatever it takes. So, I'm a man. But I can control myself, and you'd better, too." Spenser's gaze dropped into his colleague's lap. He wouldn't mind helping him out with a hand job. His own joint jumped at the thought.

* * * *

Crystal reappeared, dressed and munching on a white chocolate macadamia nut cookie. "Thanks for the diversion, guys. I need to get back to the dorm before curfew."

Spenser said, "No. You don't want to do that, to go back to a bunch of hungry women."

Tim offered, "Maybe she does. Maybe she might invite us."

Crystal held her finger up as she chewed and swallowed. "No men allowed in the dorms."

Spenser said, "So you're here to lose weight. You can't be enjoying that nasty fat laden diet and the sadistic boot camp. How about you go on our diet and exercise program, with a guarantee you'll lose more weight, tone up, and be completely sated, in every way? No deprivation, no over exertion."

"Sounds like a hedonistic orgy."

Tim nodded. "If you want it to be. We're here to pleasure you, darling." He walked over to her and ran a finger down her cheek. She trembled.

"Tell me more." She cooed.

He kissed her sweetly and looked into her eyes.

"It's simple. You have been steadily, albeit slowly, gaining weight the past few years. You have not been able to lose it. You've got ovarian syndrome, and we can fix that."

"How do you know?"

Spenser retrieved a file from the living room. "While you were bathing, we accessed your medical records online."

"How dare you!" She snatched it from him. "You had no right violating my privacy. I'll report you to the AMA and the Navy and the hotel and Homeland Security and—"

Spenser said, "Calm down, Crystal. We did it for you. Hear us out. Come on over and have a seat." He motioned to a large overstuffed arm chair with matching ottoman. Tim took her by the hand and led her over. He said, "Here, you can sit in my lap."

Crystal said, "No thank you."

Tim detoured to the bed. He managed to maneuver her to perch on the edge of it. He sat next to her, holding her hand, rubbing his thumb in a circular motion on the inside of her wrist. She tried to ignore the pleasurable sensation.

Spenser flipped through the file. "Your last well-woman check-up was on the twentieth. Just before you came down here. You complained of severe headaches on the week you're off your monthly birth control pills. The pills are no longer regulating your cycle, you complained of breakthrough bleeding, and the nurse practitioner ordered an ultrasound. No uterine polyps were found, however, you have a small cyst forming on your right ovary, which shouldn't be happening when you're taking birth control pills. That's evidence you are still ovulating; and the absence of polyps means the breakthrough bleeding is caused because the low dose pills are no longer strong enough for you."

"My gynecologist just called and said I was okay, and mentioned the cyst, and said to come back for a follow up in three months. And she changed my pills from a low dose to an average dose, I think she said it's fifty percent stronger than I was taking. And I take these for three months in a row, so I only have four periods a year now—"

Tim said, "So now you will only be bothered by the headaches that are caused from a sharp drop in estrogen when you go on the sugar pills one week every three months."

Crystal nodded. *It seems like these guys really are doctors, they just don't play them in hotels.*

Spenser asked, "When did you start the new pills?"

"Tomorrow."

"Perfect."

"Why?"

"Your hormones have been out of whack, and that caused you to secrete too much insulin. Insulin that the body doesn't need converts to fat. It also increases your cravings, so you eat more. If the average dose pill suppresses ovulation, your metabolism should right itself."

"What was that medical research business you were talking about?"

Tim said, "We have formatted a regimen that will help women such as yourself lose weight while eating what they want, which will naturally be less because of the new balance you'll have. It will be boosted by one hour of exercise daily, be it vigorous aerobic activity, weight bearing or muscle elongating. And..." he grinned.

And what?" *This all sounds too good to be true, but it's making sense and I don't want it to.*

"We think your hormones will be further balanced, and therefore more weight loss will be achieved if you receive a minimum of one *powerful* orgasm per day."

She laughed hysterically. "Sign me up."

Spenser grinned. "Seriously? You're consenting?"

"If you're on the up and up, yes I am. But I have to get back to the dorm before curfew." She walked over to the French doors.

Spenser followed her. "Let me get you a cab."

"No! I'm not allowed. We have to walk everywhere."

"Then drop out of that cult boot camp."

"I can't. I don't have money to fly home. My ticket is nonrefundable. And I can't get a refund on the boot camp either. I wouldn't have any place to stay for the rest of the time."

"Stay with us." Tim offered.

"No. What was I thinking? I've got to go."

Spenser said, "Go back to your low-carb diet and die of cravings. Go back to your injury waiting to happen exercise program. Go back to your lover girls. They can't give you the type of orgasm powerful enough to trigger weight loss."

"Eww! I don't do girls. I told you. Plain vanilla. I need a man."

Tim smiled. "And we're offering you two. Double your pleasure." He ran his hand under her hair, along the back of her neck. Crystal tried to pull away but her body failed her.

"If I stay, do you really guarantee I'll lose weight?"

Tim said, "Yes." He teased her nipples up through her shirt.

She stuck her chest out to meet his touch, then pulled away.

"No. Rosaleen. I can't do it to her."

Tim asked, "Who's Rosaleen?"

"My roommate. We're responsible for each other. The team with the greatest combined weight loss or Body Mass Index or something wins a spokesperson contract and she really, *really* wants it. Especially the free makeover. She's the one who talked me into enrolling."

Spenser said, "Go right ahead and continue with your boot camp. Make appearances. Pick one hour of exercise they offer every day and give it your all. Something different each day. Rotate through.

Their program components aren't bad, it's just as a whole they're out of their minds. Some of those morbidly obese women aren't going to survive the competition. *And I mean that, morbidly.*"

Tim asked, "How big is Rosaleen?"

"Oh, not that big. Just dumpy 'cause she's short. She's not morbidly obese."

He ran his hand down Crystal's body, cupping her breast, then slipped around back to plump her derriere. "She's not perfectly proportioned like you?"

Crystal looked into his hooded eyes and realized he meant it. As he brushed her hand against his erection, she knew how desirable she was. "Tim, take me now," she sighed.

As Tim pulled Crystal's top over her head, she kicked her shoes off and Spenser unzipped her capris from behind. Tim unfastened her exercise bra and her breasts spilled out. He gobbled one large rosy areola into his mouth. Spenser began slipping her grey cotton panties down her hips and Tim grabbed his wrist.

"No. She's mine. She wants me." He picked her up effortlessly and bounced her onto the bed.

Crystal was shocked at how strong he was. No man had ever tried to lift her before.

Spenser chucked a condom at Tim's back. He reached around, grabbed it, and ripped it open. Crystal snuggled into the mattress and splayed her legs wide open.

* * * *

Spenser hungrily inhaled her scent as he watched his friend pull the woman who saved *his life* to the edge of the bed and plunge into her. This was better than any staged porn movie. The sight of another man's cock pumping in and out, the sound of his balls slapping against her ass. The suction of their kisses and her first scream sent Spenser's mind directly to his pulsating member.

Yes, his cock felt slighted she'd picked the other guy. Yes, Tim had an extra half inch on him. But she'd only picked him because he was closest and he was sweet-talking her and rubbing her tits—those big, beautiful, perfectly formed tits, just waiting to be fucked. Spenser grabbed his cock and jerked wildly while twisting his balls with his other hand. He imagined thrusting into her tits.

She screamed again, this time in unison with Tim. As Tim's thrusts slowed to a circular after-milking, Spenser grabbed his arm. "My turn."

Tim withdrew. Spenser positioned himself to mount Crystal as he was yanked back by the shoulders. "Stop!" Tim yelled. "No rubber. Are you crazy?"

Spenser looked around in a fog, wondering where he'd left the box. He felt himself being spun around and pushed backwards onto the bed. Hot lips clamped around his cock. The most exquisite tongue caressed his sex. It didn't take long before he reached the brink. As he was about to groan "Crystal," she kissed him full on the lips. He moaned into her mouth and realized who was blowing him. It was the first time. He didn't want it to be the last. Not that he wanted it to go any further than this particular act.

They lay still on the bed, sideways, the girl in the middle. Crystal fell fast asleep. Spenser and Tim lay big eyed, each wondering what happened. Spenser finally said, "Thanks, man."

Tim said, "No problem. Anything to keep our case study uncontaminated."

Spenser liked his analogy and plausible explanation for what just innocently conspired.

"Yes, quick thinking. You got my back."

"No problem. You would have done the same for me."

Spenser lay there, envisioning Tim's prick in his mouth. It was a delicious musing. Not that it would ever happen again. It was purely a need-to-do-basis. Had to save the mission. Not to ever happen again.

Tim said, "You owe me one," and grinned.

* * * *

Miami Beach morphed into creepiness after midnight. The hotel was north of South Beach, where the road was still called Collins Avenue. If Crystal had been in the partying crowds in South Beach proper, where the road is called Washington Avenue, she wouldn't have been jumping at her shadow. She jogged her way to the Julia Tuttle Causeway and tried not looking over the bridge at the water as two convertibles sped across, shaking the structure.

All lights were out in the Jesuit dormitory building. Just the red glow of the emergency exit sign illuminated the stairwell. She used the small squeeze blue LCD light on her key chain to stumble up the musty stairs. Jumping as a commode flushed in the house mother's room, Crystal fled through the labyrinth to her room. Trying hard not to breathe, she used her little light to punch in the code.

As she closed the door behind her, she winced at the wretched wedding of cigarettes and semen. Rosaleen sat up in bed, an orange glow illuminated her contraband.

Rosaleen asked in a hoarse whisper, "Where on earth have you been? You could have called."

"How? There aren't any phones and we're not allowed to carry our cells."

"Are you all right?" Rosaleen asked.

"From the smell of things, I'd say I'm just as all right as you." Crystal's chest was tightening with little pains. "Please put that thing out."

"Fine." Rosaleen sniffed.

Oh no, here come the tears. "What's wrong, Rosaleen?"

"Dickie was here."

No shit. "I didn't realize he was in the country."

"He followed me. He wants to reconcile."

"And so you did. What does this mean now? You're leaving in the morning?" *Hope hope hope...*

"No." She blew her nose. Honked it like a fog horn. "He wants me to continue the program since, after all, he's paid for it. He said he can already see results. He was so turned on by the new firmer me." Her voice lilted.

After one day? This guy is in love. "That's wonderful, Rosaleen. I'm very happy for you."

"And just where have you been?"

"The guy that I did the Heimlich maneuver on is a doctor. He's helping me out with a different diet and exercise program."

"What kind?"

Shit. No way do I want to let her in on this. She'll ruin it for me. "Basically the same, only just one hour of exercise per day."

"But you won't lose weight like that, Crystal. No pain, no gain."

"Sure I will. And I'm certainly not passing up the chance to spend more time with a hunkalicious eligible bachelor." *Or two.*

"Oh, is it love at first sight? Dickie and I fell in love at first sight. Did I tell you the story...?" Rosaleen droned on.

Yes, Rosaleen had cut and pasted that story into so many e-mails over the years, Crystal had it memorized. Love at first sight? Hmm...maybe, but which one? Tim rocked her world. But what secrets did Spenser's penis hold?

"Beautiful story, Rosaleen. Very fairy tale-ish. I'm so happy to hear..." *and smell – gross,* "that you guys have made up. I guess you're gonna want some privacy? Does he have any problems sneaking around unnoticed?"

"Oh, not my Dickie. He's as quiet as a mouse in the heather."

Whatever heather sounded like. "Okay, then, here's the deal. Dickie can sleep here. I'll be at the hotel, in room forty-three seventeen. I'll show up at one activity each day. Something different. Actually, I might show up for one exercise and one meeting or prayer session or something. We'll gab then and catch up. And I promise I'll try my hardest not to cheat and we'll have the biggest weight loss of all the teams."

"The Patty Unger lassies are cheating! They are purging on sugar free chocolate. They have false bottoms in their makeup cases," Rosaleen gossiped.

"No!" Crystal said with great amusement. *The right and proper Patty Unger ladies have a little vice, do they?* "That stuff isn't allowed. And while it's low in carbs, it's high in calories! I don't care what the boot camp guru claims, *calories do count* on any diet!"

"Shh!"

They giggled.

* * * *

Crystal and Rosaleen slept soundly and woke up smiling as the piercing alarm opened their eyes to a new morning. They missed breakfast because Tiffany and Hilda hogged the bathroom. Pleading and pounding on the door didn't unseat them any sooner.

Crystal took a record quick shower as she breathed through her mouth and spit out bitter shampoo suds. The stench was overpowering. A sign Rosaleen's gossip was true. The P. U. girls had overloaded on the sugar free chocolate, inducing a laxative effect.

Hmm...this might be their strategy...to lose weight through dehydration. Oh, it can't be safe, though. Not with all the exertion in the heat. Crystal remembered her lovers' prediction and cringed. She said a small prayer for her competitors.

Arriving on the sand promptly at five forty-five, they slipped into the back row and assumed the yoga position *du jour*. A beautiful pink sunrise materialized over the clear aquamarine water. Two dolphins frolicked in the backdrop of a cruise ship.

Crystal enjoyed the power walking in the salt water pool, somehow akin to being in charge inside a mother's womb. She slipped out of the sauna on the pretext of potty business and winked at her roommate as she left. Rosaleen actually smiled.

After hurriedly dressing, Crystal looked both ways in the corridor and slipped past the weight room without incident. Four minutes later she knocked on their door. Spenser greeted her with a telephone to his ear. He beckoned her in and motioned to a room service cart.

Crystal heartily grabbed a white porcelain plate and piled it with scrambled eggs, bacon, sausage, and French Toast. She drizzled it in syrup. Everything.

Spenser concluded his call and poured orange juice. "What took you so long?"

"We got off to a late start because the Patty Unger girls who share our bathroom had diarrhea. They're gorging on sugar-free candy. The stretching felt so great—oh, I saw two dolphins! Have you seen any yet?"

"Yes, I can see them from my balcony."

"Really? Wow. Anyhow, I went ahead and did the power walking in the salt water pool and then the sauna. I didn't overdo it, did I?"

"How do you feel?"

"Starving!"

"You're fine then. Just think about what you're eating. If it's not delicious, don't finish it. If you feel full, stop. Don't clean your plate, young lady."

"Yes, Mother."

"I don't think you'll be calling me Mother after this evening."

"Yum." She savored the French toast. "That's right. It's your turn to give me a treatment."

"I'll treat you as the mythical goddess you are." He massaged her shoulders.

"Oh, yeah. That feels super." She gulped down a swig of orange juice and held in a small burp. She hoped he hadn't heard it.

"You know what? I think I'm full. Really. Wow."

"Fantastic. Put the fork down and step away from the room service table." He gallantly offered a hand and helped her up.

Crystal noticed he had a tie on as he slipped his uniform jacket on. "Where're you off to?"

"I'm attending a conference, remember? I've got a lecture to present in about six minutes." He pulled his sleeve over his watch.

"Well, what am I supposed to do all day?"

"Sleep. Bathe. Listen to music. Sit on the balcony and watch the dolphins. Smell the fresh roses in the boudoir."

"Really?"

"That's right. Order what you want for lunch. I might not make dinner, I need to debrief Tim before he leaves."

"Leaves?"

"He's being deployed tomorrow."

"No. You mean we only have one more night together?"

"You act like you're smitten with the guy or something." He seemed to study her response.

Spenser thinks I like Tim better. Do I? "No. It's just I thought this was a team project."

"Don't worry, goddess, I'm well equipped to see the mission through to its conclusion." He smiled as she smiled and looked him up and down.

"Well, I do get to say goodbye to Tim, right?"

"I'll ask him to stop by but he can't stay. He really does have to pack and ship out."

"Where to?"

"I can't tell you."

Crystal hoped it wasn't Iraq.

* * * *

When Spenser returned that evening, it was well past nine. He smiled to see his research subject bottoms up on his bed, dressed in a black lace teddy. *Good. She found it in the closet.* He leaned down and kissed each cheek where it peeked out of the soft fabric. As he plumped them up, she purred, "Hello, loverboy."

"Hello, goddess."

"I've been waiting for you." She rolled over and they kissed. As Spenser's lips parted, he circled them around her face, rubbing his stubble to awaken her senses. Crystal seemed to like it very much.

Spenser returned to her lips. His tongue probed deeply and he circled her gums and palate. He pulled away and looked in her eyes. They shimmered back. Green. He hadn't noticed before. Cat green. How wicked. His cock responded favorably.

"So what did you do all day?"

"Everything you suggested, plus I've been studying."

"Studying?"

"In-room movies."

Spenser looked up at the TV in the armoire. Two women were undressing one another, tearing the crotches out of each other's pantyhose. His balls

40

tightened. "So do you like that? Would you like to invite your—?"

"No. I told you. I am not interested in breasts and bottoms not my own." She looked away, blushing.

"I don't blame you. They had amateur boob jobs. Look how hard they are and wrinkled under their arms."

"The show that's coming on next. I watched it earlier. Wow. I want us to do that." She blushed again.

"Sure. Whatever my goddess desires."

"I now understand why guys like watching lesbians."

I thought she just said she wasn't interested in girls.

Crystal said, "It's a ménage a trois. Man/man/woman. The woman really gets off watching the men go at it."

"No. Absolutely not. I told you, I don't do that. I'm not gay," he said. "That's exit only, no entry allowed."

She quickly added, "Oh, not that. That grosses me out, too. I stepped onto the balcony and watched the dolphins through that scene. No. I mean the erotic foreplay between the men."

Saved by the knock at the door. It was Tim, bearing another champagne magnum. He kissed Crystal hello, slipping her the tongue and copping a feel of her breasts.

"Darling, I'm gonna miss these most of all."

Crystal smiled.

Spenser asked, "What do you want from room service?"

Crystal said, "Nothing, I'm good."

"Me too. I think we can feed off each other," Tim said.

Spenser shivered as a flash from last night replayed in his head. That was an isolated incident. Necessary so he didn't blow the case study. Tim blew him. He hoped he'd do it again. He unzipped his trousers to release the ache.

Tim slipped out of his uniform and onto the silk sheets with Crystal.

Spenser said, "Hold up a moment, cowboy. I'm riding her tonight." He joined them. "The little lady has some inspiration from the actor's guild she'd like to partake in."

"Oh, yes. Here it's starting now." Crystal said enthusiastically as she accepted a glass of champagne from Spenser. They listened to the thinly plotted dialogue, which amounted to the sexy young woman commanding her slaves to pleasure each other while she watched and played with her fake boobs.

Spenser's pulse ricocheted as he admitted to himself he very much enjoyed watching them give each other hand jobs. So much so that when the camera was on the girl, he snuck a look at Tim's equipment. Tim was stroking himself as he caught Spenser's eye. They both turned their attention to Crystal's face. In perfect correlation, they each slipped a strap off of her shoulder.

She wriggled out of the lace and Spenser threw it on top of the TV armoire. They didn't need to watch anymore. Each man suckled and kneaded a breast with both hands. She threw her head back and ran fingers through both men's hair. "Now." She softly said.

Tim and Spenser crawled next to each other and kneeled, sitting back on their legs. They looked at Crystal and she nodded as she pinched her nipples. Clumsy fondling gave way to heavy breathing and guttural moans. Tim caressed his own balls with one hand as he stroked Spenser's fat cock. Spenser moved away, worried he was on the verge. He shoved Tim down and licked his balls. Took one in his mouth and lightly suckled. Tim began jerking himself off.

Crystal said, "No. Let Spenser make you come."

With that, Spenser lowered his head over Tim's cock and the explosion came swiftly.

Thrilled with the act, ready to come himself, he rolled a condom on and gently slipped inside Crystal. Three strokes and she came. He kissed her and groaned, collapsing on top.

* * * *

Crystal felt the cool breeze from a ceiling fan kissing her relaxed body. Groggily returning to the conscious world from her intense afterglow slumber, she could hear Tim and Spenser in the living room.

"Take care of her. I can't wait to see her results. Don't let her lose more than twenty, I love those thighs."

"You and me both. I thought you were attached to her breasts..."

"I am. But I read the radiologist's report. Her mammogram showed dense fibrous tissue. Not fat. Those beauties aren't melting away no matter how much she thinks she needs to lose."

"Our Roman goddess."

"*Your* Roman goddess, Spenser. Have you told her yet?"

"Soon."

Damn. The air conditioner kicked on. It drowned out the men. She tried to drift back to sleep and dream about them complimenting her. It worked. The alarm clock woke her. Wait a minute. It wasn't a piercing blare. It was music. A clock radio.

Crystal opened her eyes and saw Spenser stretching to hit the snooze button.

"Hi." she said.

"Good morning. How do you feel?"

"Sublime. Lovely. Happy. Sated."

"Sated?" He sounded disappointed.

"Why would that surprise you? You ought to be feeling very proud of yourself, Spenser Edwards. The only man ever to please me in three strokes. Your equipment was custom fitted to mine."

He rolled her over, so she faced the window. As he kissed down her back, he said, "I bet you say that to all the sailors."

"No. There are no other sailors. No other men. Only you. After last night, I knew."

He laughed. "Don't tease."

She rolled toward him and took his morning erection in her hand. "Does this feel as if I'm teasing you?"

"Oh, yeah, baby. Tease me more."

"I mean it. I've never been so totally filled and fulfilled. Can I reenlist in your study?"

"You still have three weeks."

"Not long enough."

44

"Make up your mind." he laughed.

She took him in her mouth. He bucked, trying to stay in inside as she naughtily pulled him all the way out every other stroke. She did something with her hand on the underside of his balls that launched him.

Laying with her head on his chest, she said, "I am a firm believer in fate. Fate made Rosaleen and me meet on the Internet on the Welsh corgi e-mailing list. Fate brought us to Miami Beach and fate made you choke on the cheese. We were destined to meet, Spenser." Crystal hoped she hadn't babbled like a gold-digging blonde.

"Yes." He kissed her. Gently and possessively.

"Spenser. What does this mean? Are we a couple?"

"That depends."

"On what?" she worried.

"I don't even know what you do in your other life. Where are you from? Are you married? What's your occupation?"

"Assistant to the research librarian at the New York City public library. Single. I also breed Welsh corgis."

"In your penthouse?"

"I live in Hoboken."

"No, you don't."

"Yes, I do."

"You live in Canberra, Australia. We ship out in two weeks, Missus Edwards."

"Australia? Did you just ask me—?"

He answered by rolling on a condom and plunging his rejuvenated love between her thighs. She immediately emitted womanly moans. He slowed to a stop. "No, honey. You need to learn to draw it out. Savor the ride."

Two more thrusts and she dug her nails in his back.

He said, "Or perhaps you can just be multi-orgasmic. I'm flexible." He came.

"But two weeks? No. I can't leave in two weeks. The boot camp and contest won't be over. We can't win."

Spenser softly kissed her lips. I'm sorry, babe, but I have to get downstairs. He withdrew, stood up and removed the protection. He headed toward the bathroom.

"Wait!"

He turned toward her, his thick cock still rigid.

"I don't really want to lose a lot of weight anyhow, and even if we did win, Rosaleen would still find something to sob about...my mom can take care of my puppies. They won't even miss me at the library if I don't come back..."

"So what are you saying?"

"G'day, mate."

* * * *

Crystal took the freight elevator down to the basement and wandered through corridors cluttered with white laundry carts and low hanging pipes. She found an exit and shoved the door open. She was startled by a brown uniformed maintenance man carrying a large barrel of something or other. Instantly smiling, she held to door for him and said, "Good morning."

He grunted and lumbered down the hallway.

Crystal held the door as it closed, pressing it shut. She swung her arms as she climbed the loading dock ramp, then wove through the parking lot, scanning for any signs of the boot camp sergeants or the stinky ladies. *If they find out I've been sleeping upstairs in the hotel, Rosaleen and I will be tossed out of the competition. The competition...I can't do this to poor Rosaleen.* A wave of shame passed over her, pausing in her empty stomach. *Missed breakfast. Shoot. Well, I'll make up for it at lunch, I'll order room service.* Crystal smacked her forehead. *Yeah, go ahead and pig out at lunch, idiot. You skipped breakfast so your body is gearing up for starvation mode, slowing your metabolism.*

She stepped out from behind a yellow, blooming hibiscus bush and onto the sidewalk in front of the hotel. She pulled her hair into a ponytail and fastened it with the elastic band she had around her wrist.

Crystal entered through the revolving lobby doors and headed down the grand staircase to the mezzanine level where the gym was located. She smiled at the perky size-zero attendant with a clipboard and said, "Levitan."

The skinny Minnie scanned a list and made a check mark. "All righty, Miss Levitan, you are scheduled for thirty-two minutes on the elliptical today." She glanced at the big-faced clock near the ceiling and said, "Hurry, you're almost late."

Crystal spied Rosaleen and sprinted over, hopping onto the contraption, pulling something in her ankle. "Ouch!"

Rosaleen panted, "You okay?"

"Yep. I'm more than okay," Crystal said as she shuffled the machine to a slow start and keyed in a fat burning program.

"This is the best thing that's ever happened to me. I'm firming up and finding a new peace. Dickie and I have never been happier."

Crystal pulled back hard on the poles, then pushed just as hard, determined to get the most of this workout. *How am I going to tell her?*

Rosaleen ran a finger underneath the yellow sweatband holding her orange Methuselah 'do out of her eyes. She grabbed the pole as her stride stumbled.

"You okay?"

"Marvelous. What a grand day to be in love."

"I agree."

Rosaleen turned toward Crystal. "Are things magical between you and the sailors?"

"Sailor. One is gone."

"Ah, so you've made your choice. Tell me all about him. Tall, dark, handsome and charming no doubt?"

"Of course. And I understand about Dickie now."

"What do you mean?"

"Love at first sight. Well, not at first sight exactly. Well, now no. After I did the Heimlich maneuver on him and got a good look, my heart did go pitter patter."

The machine beeped at Crystal. She saw a red LED message running across the screen. Speed up. Raise your pulse rate. *Yeah yeah yeah.* She picked the pace back up.

"He asked me to marry him!"

Rosaleen squealed. Hilda pedaled next to her as she breathlessly said, "Would you keep it down? Some of us are trying to concentrate."

"Aye," Rosaleen said.

"Keep it down? Concentrate on what?" Crystal asked. She looked across her partner and at the row of exercisers. They were all wearing headphones and craning their necks up at television monitors. QVC was having a jewelry sale.

Jewelry. Wedding ring. Engagement ring. Marriage. Husband. Kids? Australia? What am I getting myself into?

Rosaleen slowed to a stop as Crystal's machine beeped through the cool down and she completed her program a few seconds later. They accepted plush lavender towels from Miss Skinny Minnie and headed into the ladies locker room and sauna.

Hilda and Tiffany were inside, huddled in conversation debating the merits of the new formula for hair balm.

Rosaleen sat on a wooden bench as Crystal dipped a ladle into a bucket of water and drizzled it over the hot rocks. *Hot rocks. Spenser's hot rocks. Oh, to drizzle saliva over his hot rocks.*

Moisture rushed to her feminine zone, not that it wasn't already soaked with sweat. She sat next to her friend and whispered, "Rosaleen. Spenser ships out in two weeks and I'm going with him. We're getting married and I need to call my mom and tell her to take care of the puppies for me. I'm moving to Australia and I'm so sorry I won't be able to finish the competition with you, but you're doing so well and I'm just so tickled you and Dickie have finally gotten to a good point—"

Rosaleen let out a blood curdling wail. "No! You can't do this to me! We had a deal, an agreement, a pact, a friendship!"

The make-up ladies huffed by, glaring at them. Their suite mate Hilda said, "What's wrong? Can't take the heat? Drop out of the competition then, Crystal Bee. Crystal Ball. Crystal wrecking ball." Tiffany laughed.

Crystal glared at them. "This is none of your concern. Beat it."

"Yeah? Who's gonna make me?"

What the hell am I doing, baiting Two-Ton Tillie into a cat fight? Why, all she'll have to do is sit on me and I'll be asphyxiated.

"Just as I thought. Too much of a sissy. Can't take the heat." The two P. U. ladies cackled as they left the sauna. The door slammed shut behind them. A piece of paper floated to the floor. Rosaleen sniffled and picked it up.

"A sugar-free milk chocolate toffee bar!"

"Hippo." Crystal took a lavender towel from the stack near the door and tried to wipe Rosaleen's nose with it. She shoved her away. Crystal tried to hug her but Rosaleen went limp.

"All right. I'll work something out. I'll fly back in time for the weigh in or something."

"That will cost a fortune! And they'll notice you've been absent. You can't leave."

"Sure I can. The last week we're on our own, anyhow. Page seventy-three of the syllabus. Didn't you read and memorize it?"

Rosaleen snatched the towel and blew her nose into it. "Aye, I think you are right. But if you're not exercising and eating right, you'll gain all your weight back. And probably swell up from the flight. Water weight will kill our chances."

"Passport!" Crystal gasped. "I don't have a passport. I can't go anywhere unless I can get an emergency passport. Yeah. I'll do that. No. Wait. What's my emergency? I have to go to Australia immediately so I can make love with a sailor morning, noon, and night on a Navy ship."

"You can't go onboard ship with him."

"Why not?"

"The dependents go separately. He'll be on duty on the ship, silly lass."

"Yeah, and how do you know this?"

"My old dad was in the Royal Navy. We've traveled the world."

"No, maybe the U.S. Navy is different..."

"Maybe so, but I highly doubt it." Rosaleen smiled, yanked off her glasses and dried her eyes with an untouched corner of the towel. "We've got that settled. You can't go with him so you'll just have to finish out the competition, then apply for the passport, get your affairs in order in New Jersey, return your library books then kiss your puppies and mummy goodbye."

* * * *

Crystal joined the boot campers in the Palm Ballroom for lunch. Suckling pig and celery sticks. As the Cuban chef split open the pork belly, Crystal's eyes were fixed in a staring contest with the poor pig's. Of course he won. When she blinked she thought about his life. He grew big and fat, they slaughtered him and stuck an apple in his mouth, skewered him and roasted him on a spit. She didn't want to grow bigger and fatter. And die with an apple in her mouth as they skewered her and roasted her on a spit. She wanted to lose weight, tone up, and win this competition, damn it.

There had to be a way to keep Spenser in Miami Beach. He could come down with the chicken pox. Or mumps. No, not mumps. That does something to grown men's *cajones* and they were too valuable to mess up. What else was highly contagious that the Navy wouldn't want him in close quarters on a ship with a thousand other men and women?

Men and women.

Spenser is going to be aboard ship in close quarters with sassy Navy and Marine women! They'll brush by him in the corridors, rubbing their pert breasts up against him. No. Not if she could help it.

Why, Crystal Bee Levitan-soon-to-be-Edwards, I do believe you are jealous.

* * * *

When Crystal returned to Spenser's hotel room, he was lying on the couch reading a stack of documents. He held his pointing finger up and said, "Almost done. One moment, beautiful." Then he dropped his finger and lifted the middle one, grinning as he finished the paragraph.

"I'll be waiting." She walked into the bedroom and opened the closet. His uniforms were neatly pressed and hanging. She peeled her exercise clothes off, letting them pile on the floor. Spying the classic white sailor's cap on the shelf, she donned it and the hamster on the wheel of her brain began running. She could dress up like a sailor, sneak onto the ship and hide out in his room. They could make mad passionate love and no one would ever know. Wait. What if he had roommates? Shoot. *I'll bet they are packed like tiramisu in bunks, tucked into odd voids of the bowels in the ship.* She sighed.

Crystal heard his belt unbuckle as he whipped it out of the loops. He snapped it. She swallowed.

"Sailor, you're out of uniform. You know what the punishment for that is?"

Crystal turned to him. "No. Absolutely not. No BDSM."

"Do not talk back to your superior, sailor."

"Perhaps we can make a deal?"

"What sort of deal?"

"I'll let you do to me or I'll do to you the first act that is on the pay-per-view at the moment we switch it on." Crystal thought this was a pretty safe idea, since the shows always started with some talking, then either the girl went down on the guy or he played with her breasts.

Spenser grabbed the remote from the bed and clicked it. The hotel information channel came on. He flipped to "Coupling Up".

The immediate scene was of an exquisitely chiseled guy kneeing on the floor in front of a sofa. A naked woman clutched her knees and moaned as he tongued her anus.

"No! Not that. Why is this show in progress? It always starts when you select the channel."

"I was watching it earlier." He peeled his clothes off and yanked the duvet off the bed. He reached for her hand. She again said, "No. Un unh," as he gently circled his thumb around the inside of her wrist.

He tugged her onto the bed. She looked at the TV. The camera panned to another sofa where a second couple was lying on their side, watching the first. The camera zoomed in on the second guy inserting his cock into her rear end as she masturbated.

Crystal's heart pounded. She wanted no part of that, but she couldn't help noticing moisture pooling down there as her privates swelled in anticipation of her lover.

Spenser slipped his hand between her legs and the juices gushed out. She rolled her nipples between her fingers and closed her eyes.

"Do you want me to pleasure you here?" He circled a finger around her ass cheeks, not quite touching the entry. She trembled.

"No. Plain vanilla."

"Good. Your orgasm wouldn't be as strong by manual stimulation. You need my cock to rock your g-spot." He kissed her, shoving his tongue deep into her mouth, entwining it with his furiously as he shoved a finger inside her vagina and groaned. Two fingers. His thumb worked her clit. Just as she was on the brink, he buried his cock inside her and she wrapped her legs around his ribs. A wave of pleasure over took her as the room spun. The ceiling fan was a white blur, like a ship's propeller. Her climax was long and hard. As her shuddering ended, Spencer kissed her forehead. He slowed his thrusts down as he kissed her nipples.

Crystal squirmed.

"What's the matter?"

"Hypersensitive."

"Of course. After that number six on the Richter scale. Relax. Close your eyes. Come for me again."

She imagined herself with him aboard ship, making love surrounded by other hunky shirtless sailors swabbing the poop deck, all around them. Now they were pantless, too. Just black boxer briefs with yummy bulges. Wait. Now they were doing a dance routine from an old Kirk Douglas movie. She slightly shook her head.

"What's wrong now?"

"Nothing. Just trying to focus." She concentrated fully on the friction between his penis and her vagina and clitoris. Squeezing his muscular ass, she guided him in and out, in and out, in and out. Faster. Faster. Faster. She screamed. Screamed so loud she embarrassed herself. As her contractions subsided, he slowed his thrusts and kissed her, giggling.

"What's so funny?"

"My plain vanilla girl is a wild animal."

"Well, what do you expect? I've never been copulated like this before."

"Poor thing." He giggled again.

"Hey, come on now. It's no time for humor." She silenced him as she pulled him down by the triceps and kissed him like she meant it.

He let himself go and she thought he'd drive her through the headboard, the wall, and into the next room as he pumped into her like mankind depended on his seed surviving.

As he screamed, "Oh, Crystal!" and launched his seed, it occurred to Crystal there was no barrier.

He buried his head in her shoulder with a contented smile. She wiggled out from under him.

"What's wrong?" he asked.

She looked at his glistening naked cock and pointed to it. "No protection."

"Yeah, so? You're on the Pill. If you're worried about disease, I assure you I'm clean. As a matter of fact, I've never gone without a raincoat before. Nope. No need to. I know you're healthy, and since you're the last woman I'll ever be making love to, might as well enjoy every inch of our love."

She turned onto her side and stared out the open curtains. The red lights of a freighter in the distance caught her attention. "I can't go with you to Australia. Because with the stupid terror regulations, I can't dress up like a sailor and play Lucille Ball and sneak onto the ship and press the big red button that says don't press, and if I don't make love with you every day, I won't lose weight. And if I don't lose weight, I'll end up downstairs in the sauna with an apple stuffed in my mouth and stinky painted ladies will roast me on a spit. But most of all, I can't let Rosaleen down."

She rolled over and looked at him. They both burst into laughter, though hers had a few tears.

He shoved her head on his chest and held her tightly. "I'm not going to even try to analyze what you just said. I'm sorry I didn't go into details of our deployment with you. I've filed the paperwork to get married, but I need your birth certificate before we can get the license. Can your mother Fed-Ex it to you?"

"Mom! I'm denying my poor mother from seeing her only child get married. She'll have a fit! She probably won't mail it to me for spite, to halt the nonsense."

"Nonsense?" He let go of her head.

She rolled over and hoisted up on her elbows, facing him. "She'll say it's nonsense."

"So invite her down for the civil ceremony."

"When?"

"How about tomorrow?"

"No. She won't fly."

"Will she take the train? No, that would be way too slow. How about a bus?"

"She goes on road trips with her friend Kat all the time. They'll drive. Kat and Mom can be our witnesses."

"Okay. How long will it take for them to drive here?"

"From New Jersey? Two days tops. They both have lead feet. Mom drives a red Corvette."

Spenser giggled again. "I can't wait to meet my mother-in-law."

"Careful what you wish for..." Crystal sat up. "Wait a minute. You never told me my itinerary."

"Do you have a passport?"

"No." She lamented.

"We can get one expedited, but it will still take a good three weeks to a month. You can fly over on a commercial carrier and meet me in Canberra. I'm in line to get officer's quarters on base, so we can set up house keeping right away."

"But how can I lose weight without you making love to me?"

He rubbed his whiskers. "The old fashioned way, sweetheart. Calories in and calories burned. You'll have to step up your exercising and lay off the desserts."

She groaned.

He popped up and took her hands in his. "You know, this love-at-first-sight business has spun us so fast in the centrifuge that we've forgotten something very important that all engaged couples have to do. It's the law."

"What?"

"I love you."

Crystal smiled. "I love you, too."

They kissed and made love all night long.

* * * *

Rosaleen and Crystal had nothing to eat or drink after dinner the night before the final weigh and measure-in. Miss Skinny Minnie wouldn't let them see where the scale balanced, she made them stand backwards. The calipers pinched and prodded them but they got through it unscathed. Assembled back inside the Palm Ballroom, Crystal sat in the rigid chair, tugging on the waistband of her jeans, they kept slipping down. She looked over at Rosaleen's orange pedicure in her flip-flops and grabbed her sweaty hand. They bowed their heads, wishing the boot camp commandant would hurry up with all of her thanking the VIPs and announce the winning team.

"We had a record seventeen teams drop out of the competition. Some sort of intestinal virus swept through. We wish them a speedy recovery and they are welcome to join us here again next year."

Crystal tutted. *Intestinal virus, yeah right. More like the contraband chocolate did a number on them.* Rosaleen's fingernails were digging into Crystal's knuckles. She gritted her teeth as the third and second runners up were announced. Not them.

"And the winners of this year's competition are from Peterhead, Scotland, Ms. Rosaleen Dalrymple, and her partner, from Hoboken, New Jersey, Ms. Crystal Levitan."

Gasps, hisses, and applause carried the girls up to the stage. They shook hands with the dignitaries and each accepted a clear Lucite trophy in the shape of a suckling pig with a red plastic apple in his mouth. They burst into fits of giggles and happy tears.

* * * *

Canberra, Australia

"I now pronounce you man and wife. You may kiss your bride," said the Navy chaplain.

Spenser lifted the gossamer veil and smiled at his wife, kissing her possessively. Crystal wanted the moment to last forever. She stifled a whimper as he pulled away and offered her his arm. She took it and smiled at Rosaleen, stunning in her gorgeous red maid-of-honor dress. Crystal couldn't get over what the transformation the boot camp and the make-over had done for her pal. Gone was the unruly Methuselah hair, now replaced by a slick chic bob. Laser surgery corrected her vision so she could ditch the eyeglasses. They'd even gone dress shopping with her and found a formal gown that accentuated her newly toned curves, and what a relief it was to see her in closed toe shoes!

Rosaleen handed Crystal her bouquet of white roses. Dr. and Mrs. Spenser Edwards promenaded down the aisle, then into an adjoining Sunday school classroom to wait for the guests to assemble outside for the throwing of the bouquet. The best man followed them in and shut the door.

"May I kiss the bride?" Tim asked.

Spenser grinned as he motioned toward her and said, "Just make sure that's all you do. She's all mine...on our wedding night."

Crystal was relieved her parents and the reverend didn't witness this sensual kiss. She finally pushed him away. "That's enough now."

He whispered, "Can I stop by tomorrow and kiss the groom, too?"

She shot a look at her husband and said, "It's up to him."

The reverend knocked on the door. "We're ready."

Tim left first.

Crystal and Spenser emerged on the marble church steps to greet the small group of close family and friends who cheered and wished them well. Dickie was tying tin cans and streamers to the rear bumper of the rented limo, much to the irritation of the driver. Crystal spun and threw her bouquet. Rosaleen stumbled as she dove for it, right into the arms of a buff young sailor. He laid a lip lock on her. Dickie took a swing at him and instantly others joined the brawl.

Spenser guided his giggling bride down the stairs and into the back of the limo.

Devil's Night
Meg Winston

Chapter One

"I love you," he said, and Cat Harrison fucking laughed. Because really, what else was she supposed to do? An exiled best friend making big, foolish, emotional declarations he couldn't possibly mean...No, laughter was the best of her choices. The worst involved thumping him *hard* and telling him what he could do with himself.

Then, miraculously, there were handcuffs. A scowl that suited his gorgeous face but shouldn't have, a lunge that could have been for kissing or tickling or wrestling for the remote a year ago but, instead, turned out to be for pinning. Then her arms were behind her, wrists caught in his hand, and a pair of rather ominous clicks that didn't worry her until he'd pulled away.

She tried to follow, to sit upright again and regain some poise in the face of Demon Drew Benedict and his big declaration, and found she couldn't. Because...handcuffs. He'd cuffed her to her *coffee table*. This was awkward.

God, she should never have let him in.

* * * *

Plan A, just telling her and hoping she'd be reasonable, died a quick and painful death when she laughed, taking with it his ability to get through plans B and C without lashing out. Love fucking hurt no matter what he did, and Drew Benedict wasn't much for pain.

Hence the cuffs. Captain Nasty's Fuzz Cuffs of Fury probably weren't ideal romantic props, but theirs wasn't an ideal romance. It had taken him too long to realize how he felt, and there was too much history of being scared shitless at giving up his overactive sex life, even if it was for her. Being with Cat the way she deserved meant responsibility. Commitment. Passing up hot blondes and adventurous redheads for the rest of his life in favor of the best friend who'd cut him out of hers. Better, he'd decided, to leave her be and hope it went away.

He'd been an idiot.

God, she was gorgeous cuffed and furious. Must be some measure of his oft-cited depravity. Watching her fight with the fuzz cuffs was turning him on so much. Fire in her eyes, venom on her lips, curves dancing as she writhed.

He shifted in his seat, already atrociously hard at the thought of what she'd hidden beneath those hideous sweats. At what he planned to do to her sweet, lush body.

"Cat," he said. She tried to kill him with her glare. "Wild Cat, if you don't quit that, I'll have to strip you."

She hissed at him, proof positive she'd more than earned her nickname despite her sweetness-and-light persona. Twenty years of friendship had given him the inside track. No, not just friendship. Best friendship. Forever.

And in an hour or so—provided he could keep his pants on that long—lovers.

He meant that forever, too.

Given how long he'd wanted to get to this moment, Drew thought he could be patient.

"Didn't I tell you never to darken my door again?"

He shrugged like her pronouncement two months earlier hadn't fucked him up but good.

"Knew you didn't mean that." He dismissed the death promised in her eyes.

She snorted. Indelicate and, he imagined, indicative. No sweet little kitten as everyone assumed — she was nothing so domesticated. A right hellcat.

"The hell I didn't."

"Then why'd you let me in?"

She twitched, so cool and calculated his heart flipped again.

"Maybe I wanted to keep you here until Luke showed up for another swing at you." She trailed off, letting him imagine her standing by while that slick drip she'd dated broke his nose.

Fair was fair, he supposed. Though it was hardly his fault the drip had been a bleeder.

"And if I'm attached to my nose as is?"

"Then you shouldn't have come."

He raised one brow. Knew it was cocky and arrogant and simply didn't care.

"It's Devil's Night, Wild Cat. Where else would I be?"

* * * *

God, he was killer gorgeous. That drop-to-your-knees-and-fuck-me face, those impossibly dark eyes. Twenty years and she'd never pinned the color

65

precisely to her own satisfaction. Navy, maybe. Royal blue in some lights, endless night in others. Dark and depthless and dangerous.

Eyes to make a woman beg. An ass to match. A wet dream of a body, carved by gritty hours on the rugby pitch, grimy days on the soccer field, and sweaty years on the hockey rink, all broad shoulders and long muscles and sketches of dark fur over sun-kissed skin. Bloody crime he was clothed. Men that hot should have to live naked.

In retrospect, he'd been sexy as fuck at five years old, sitting across from her in the coat room, both of them trapped on milk crates for their crimes against the kindergarten class rules. Though clearly, at five and counting, she hadn't recognized it as "sexy". That clobbered her at fifteen when the hormones kicked in. She'd fallen for him then, *hard*, conveniently just in time for his transformation to Demon Drew, king of the first date fucks.

As far as she knew, she was the only girl at Central High he hadn't seen fit to date. Instead, he'd considered her a friend, probably one of his best. Every detention she'd ever had, every punishment she'd ever served, had been directly related to Drew Benedict.

They'd survived twenty years on a pair of simple rules: she'd ignore his blatant sex appeal and he'd ignore her size. She knew the state of her own BMI just fine, thanks, and she had her mother around to remind her should she forget. The last thing she needed was one more person pointing it out. For his part, he'd had girls hanging off him since elementary school and she figured it did his ego a world of good to have one female in his life who *didn't* drool at the sight of him. She'd held up her end of the bargain, but two months earlier he'd broken his. Rearranged the face of her current boyfriend, the only guy willing to date someone euphemistically considered Rubenesque.

Right after he'd used the dreaded F word.

So goodbye friendship, hello bitter life without Drew.

Yet there he was. On her couch, watching her fight with her damned handcuffs and her damned coffee table. At the rattle of cuffs against wrought iron coffee table, Cat cursed her sentimentality.

She should never have let him in.

Then he quoted their tradition at her and she saw red.

"Don't start. I know what day it is."

Like she could possibly forget. Devil's Night meant Drew and Cat running loose in the streets, soaping windows in the business district or throwing toilet paper over the neighbor's trees. Blowing a week's allowance on eggs and pelting every car on her block. She couldn't pitch worth a damn, but thanks to Demon Drew she could lob a jack-o-lantern half a block.

Now, apparently, it meant cuffing her to a table and smirking from just out of kicking range. Impossibly sexy fucker.

"Surprised to see me, Catharine?" His voice, smooth and thick, rolled over her like fog. She felt the vibration of it inside, a tickle through her innards like a caress of her uterus.

Fuck. Shouldn't be feeling him there. Not when he couldn't care less about her girly bits.

"Not really. You're like a bad penny, Andrew. Can't shake you for trying."

He looked her over long and slow, like her sweats weren't there and he was merely fine-tuning his attack. If he thought he could eye her like that, picture her Buddha belly and waistless frame naked for his own amusement, he could fuck himself.

"You're not really trying, though, are you, Catharine?"

She tried to kick him. Failed, and wondered how she'd blown that.

He chuckled. "See, babe, if you'd honestly meant that, you wouldn't have missed."

Impossible to sit properly, given the cuffs. No give to them at all, little more than an inch of chain at best. She pulled, testing the boundaries. Tried again in a snap as though she could spring herself if only she pulled hard enough. Such a pain in the ass.

"Come a little closer," she said, and shock of shocks, he did. Never would have expected him gullible, but maybe he'd forgotten why he called her Wild Cat.

Before she could aim another kick, he leaned in and touched her hair. Rubbed it between his fingers like he hadn't seen the dark curls a million times before, which made her snort again.

Irrelevant that it made her nipples hard, made her cream her sexless sweats. Chalk that up to things he didn't need to know.

Irresponsibly sexy fucker.

She tried to pull away but really, where the hell was she going? She rattled the chain on her cuffs again in protest.

Given her precarious position, he'd trapped her there under him and every estrogen-fueled cell in her screamed that he'd settled into a sex position of sorts.

Not that there'd actually be sex. She was in sweats, for Christ's sake, and he was Demon Drew, king of the first date fucks. Undoubtedly not there to date her.

So she tried to wiggle out from under him.

* * * *

God, she'd almost kneed him. The only bony part of her and she'd tried to jab it into the hardest part of him. He wasn't much for pain in the bedroom, but somehow Wild Cat's efforts to unman him only strengthened his resolve.

Proof positive she was his girl.

When he got her naked, he'd make damned sure she understood the importance of playing nice with the sexy bits. He imagined pinching her nipples, nipping at her clit, and figured he could impart that lesson, no problem.

"That wasn't very nice," he said, moving in closer. If he moved a fraction of an inch, their noses would touch. If he breathed right, those ripe tits would rub his chest. He sucked in deep and found half the thrill gone because she'd worn sweats thicker than they looked.

"Let me up, you fucker."

The lack of heat amused him. He caught her expression and revised the thought. There was heat there, all right, just not the sort she'd been trying to project. No anger, just passion.

God, he could fuck her raw right there. Just peel down those terrible sweatpants and ram her hard, until she shook and shuddered and screamed for intervention from a deity or two because the pleasure was so intense.

Her lips parted. Silently screamed, "Do me with your mouth." He seriously considered taking her up on her offer.

"You want up, Wild Cat?" She nodded. A twitch of a motion, but a nod all the same. "Really?" Another nod, just as faint. "It's not that simple." He traced a finger down her face solely to feel the warm silk of her skin. Found his finger tracing the curve of her mouth as a smile curved his. "You want up, Wild Cat, it'll cost you.'

"What?"

God, even if he couldn't see the interest in her eyes, he'd have heard it in her voice. "Way I see it, Wild Cat, you're kind of stuck here, aren't you? Tied up pretty, just waiting to play. You want to play, don't you?" She shuddered once. He wondered if she'd look as wide-eyed and lost when she came. "Because I want to play. With you." He couldn't stop himself from looking down at the horrid gray cotton covering her fantastic breasts any more than he could stop the wicked fantasies those tits created. It took real effort to look back at her face so he didn't, just stared at her chest and touched her mouth and spoke. "I think you want to play, too, don't you, Wild Cat? Get nice and sweaty with me, huh? Spread for me nice and wide, let me taste every inch of you.

Your ass, baby. Your tits. God, I have these dreams about your tits. Love those dreams, babe. So fucking hot. I can hardly wait to show you all the dirty, nasty things I want to do to your body, Wild Cat. Would you like me to?"

She didn't say a thing but he heard her breath clear as hell and it picked up, grew heavier and faster with each image he sketched. He got harder. She got hotter.

He thought maybe they'd just attack each other.

Then she rattled her wrists again. "Andrew."

"Tell me you love me," he said, low and quiet and solemn as hell. "Tell me you want this. Or…"

"Or?"

His eyes lifted. Locked on hers and held, steady, strong and so damned hungry for her, he couldn't think.

"Or make me believe you don't."

Chapter Two

"Hit on someone your own size."

His gaze raked over her body, hit every luscious curve along the way. Harder now that she wasn't stretching out anymore, but not impossible. Not with the right motivation.

Fuck, wasn't he motivated in spades?

"Make me."

She rattled her wrists and glared black, vicious death in his direction. "Let me go and I will."

"Ah ah ah, Wild Cat. What did I just finish telling you?" He twitched his forefinger like a metronome just to see that delicious souring of her face. She had the greatest lips ever. Soft and full, curved all to hell and wide enough to spread nicely.

Some mouths were just made for oral.

"You're a dickhead and I'm fully entitled to kick your ass when I get up?" She asked it sweetly, capped it with a quick bat of her eyelashes that nearly floored him.

God, how the hell had he gotten so lucky? Curves like that, cleavage to her fucking collarbone, legs nearly as high, and what his grandpa would have called serious pushin' cushion. If he could have assembled his fantasy girl from scratch, he'd have come up with Cat Harrison. That she had a saucy mouth, a dirty mind, and a talent for trouble was icing on the hormonal cake.

She was all sugar when her eyes dipped, all spice when she looked up at him again.

"The only way I'm letting you up is if you convince me you don't love me, too." He reached down to run his fingers over the curve of her cheek, enjoying the way her mouth snarked but her eyes clouded with confusion. "That you don't want me. Tell me you don't want me and I'll let you up." Her mouth tensed as though she planned to speak, so he cut her off. "You have to mean it, though. I'll know if you lie."

She fixed her lips tight. "You're not irresistible, you know."

"Prove it."

He pushed his finger against the crease of her mouth until she gave enough to let him in. Wasn't really surprised when she latched on with a cautionary clamp of teeth. *A biter*. He shuddered.

Then she sucked him. Swirled her tongue over the pad of his fingertip, pursed her lips around him and drew him in to the second joint.

Oh, God. She was fellating his finger. He suspected it as she started but by the time she bobbed her head ever-so-slightly to run the smooth, slick inside of her mouth over the rough skin on his finger, he was sure.

It hit like a shot of testosterone and, despite his carefully laid plans for them both, he struggled to keep from yanking off his pants and hers. He could fuck her right then, easy. Just pound into her until the worst of the uncomfortable erection disappeared and he'd busted a nut buried deep in her sweet, tight kitty.

If the daze in her eyes was any indication, she'd bust a nut, too. He sniffed. Tried to make it look cool and calculated so she wouldn't know he was searching for the unmistakable scent of willing woman.

Mother of God, what had he been thinking? Wild Cat, handcuffed to the coffee table at the end of her couch, nothing but her hanging-around-the-house sweats and his wear-em-everywhere jeans between him and the best piece he'd had, ever. No way she wouldn't be the best. Not when they'd both waited so long for it. Not when they'd clearly stumbled into love somehow.

"God, Wild Cat." He groaned it. Curled the hand she wasn't mock-blowing around the back of her head so he could fist her hair and regain some sort of control.

Pulling that luscious mouth off his hand was the single hardest thing he'd ever done. The only thing that even came close had been the night of the Luke Incident, and two months later, Drew still wasn't quite over *that* yet.

He'd been six months into a hardcore, unshakable crush by then, well and truly smitten, and he'd spent that whole night watching her slime of a boyfriend eye every skirt in the bar but her. Nearly swallowed his tongue when she'd walked in that night, criminal cleavage and a skirt just begging to be hiked high and out of the way. That bright smile, eyes heavy-lidded as the alcohol got to her. She'd laughed at everything, just about mauled him in hello, then introduced him to the jackass on her arm.

He honestly could have taken out Luke's teeth before he'd ordered his first drink. The depth of his own jealousy unsettled him, but he'd watched them both all night anyway. Totally ignored the rest of the bar, despite Cat's efforts to point out potential playmates for him.

Would that Luke had done the same. But no. So while Drew'd done his best to drown his temper, tune out the world, and keep his hands to himself, Luke had done precisely the opposite.

He'd thought nothing could be worse than that, knowing the guy who had the only woman worth having wasn't fucking bright enough to deserve her.

Then she'd gone to the bathroom, he'd gone outside for some air, and Luke had trailed him. Opened his big, stupid mouth and pushed every button Drew had. Stopping at one punch, that had been fucking heroic.

Having Cat catch him, having her ban him from her life, had been fucking brutal.

Walking away then had nearly killed him but he'd done it for her, so she wouldn't get hurt worse. He'd stayed away for two months, given her time to sort herself out.

Fuck this. Time's up.

So he kissed her.

* * * *

He assaulted her mouth. It started as a kiss, just the regular, ordinary first-base kiss, and for a heartbeat or two she settled back to let him do it. His mouth was criminal. Hard and determined. No light coaxing, no half-hearted effort at a little tongue, just straight-for-the-good stuff.

Pre-sex, that kiss. No mistaking it. She spread her legs, let him in as close as he wanted to get and for a few glorious minutes, hours, moments, however long they were kissing, she had his hard body right against hers.

Just exactly where she wanted it.

If he could break her only rule, damn it, she could break his.

His erection pushed into her stomach, a reminder that there was more than just this ass-kicker kiss in their future. She shifted again, wanting him there between her thighs, pushing deep and rocking.

Not that he was actually doing anything about it. Had her soaking and half-crazy to strip him down and explore, and all bright boy wanted to do was kiss her. Bastard.

She angled her pelvis then pushed it up, lifting her hips to grind against his cock through their clothes. If she had to settle for a dry hump until he'd gotten off his sexy ass, she'd do it. Just…God…if she could just get a little clit friction going on, she'd come right there on her couch, semi-clothed and kissing him.

She wouldn't even feel bad about it. Sexy fucker.

* * * *

He lifted his mouth off hers and half-slumped on her while he caught his breath. He thought maybe she'd kill him if they ever got naked.

Cat tried to wrap her arms around him, maybe prod a little. Possibly even start the getting-him-naked bit.

Rediscovered her tied-up-with-nowhere-to-go state and fumed all over again.

"Uncuff me."

He lifted his head, which took way too much energy. God, he could just lie on her for hours. Days. She was soft in all the right places and damn, but he wanted to savor.

Funny, that she hadn't gone searching for the safety releases yet. Smart cookie usually, which led to a few interesting possibilities. Either he'd worked her up so much she hadn't had time to consider it yet or — and this was the option he preferred — she knew they were there and chose to ignore them. If she had sense enough to argue with him, why wouldn't she have sense enough to check for a way out?

Heady stuff, that she might want to be right there doing just that.

"Ready to tell me what I want to hear?"

Her mouth was all swollen, her face all flushed. He licked his lips and caught the sweet-and-sour taste of her all over again. Rubbed his denim-covered erection into her soft belly again in response.

"Get off me, you dolt."

A wicked grin curved his mouth, lifted one corner higher than the other. "Now, now, Catharine," he said low and taunting, his fingers playing with the neck of her hoodie. "Is that any way to talk to your best friend?"

* * * *

She held her breath as he tugged down her zipper. The rasp was so loud. How could one small bit of metal sound so loud? How could it be taking him this long to tug the zip from breastbone to waist? Christ on a cross, he was going slowly on purpose. Making her crazy, as promised.

"Doesn't take ten years to get that thing off me, Benedict."

"Getting impatient on me, honey?"

"Andrew." Her eyes narrowed. Her pulse pounded, her heart beating so fast he could no doubt feel it through the grey cotton knit of her sweatshirt.

Drew licked his lips. Turned his attention back to dragging down her zipper.

She ground her teeth, a reflex to the frustration simmering low and consuming her. She knew what he didn't—precisely what he'd find under that grey cotton. She dreaded his reaction as much as she craved it.

In this, there would be no halfway. His reaction would either set the night off like fireworks or kill it flat.

So, heart lodged mid-throat, hands limp over her head and stomach sucked in as much as she could maintain, she waited for him to blow this. If he broke her rule again, they'd identify his body through dental records.

Instead, he swore. As he pulled the zipper apart and spread her hoodie to expose her torso, his expression slackened. She'd kill to see his eyes clearly. Wanted to read his reaction there, where he wouldn't be able to hold a lie.

He stared at her chest like he'd just found God and for all she wiggled under him to draw his attention back, he wouldn't budge.

"You're trying to make me nuts, aren't you?" So low, his voice. So quiet. And Christ, such reverence.

"It's just clothes," she said, aware of how strange it must seem, how much it gave away of herself that he'd found this part of her. Who else put on skanky underthings for a night at home alone? Why not just broadcast she'd had some quality time planned with her vibe?

"It's a corset." His eyes lifted to hers and the severity of the situation hit her then. He'd turned her on with a kiss. She'd blown his mind with a corset. She wanted to think that put them at equal, but she suspected he'd disagree.

"Just clothes," she repeated, praying he wouldn't touch her pants for a bit. God knew how he'd react if he did.

"Expecting company?"

"Yeah. The new boy toy. He'll be along momentarily to kick your ass."

He laughed then, but the sound strangled itself. "Christ, Wild Cat." He kissed her again, a brush of his mouth over hers that ended way too soon and contained not nearly enough sex in it for her taste. "Me," he said, dazed. "You were expecting me."

She snorted, uncomfortable at his perception. "Full of yourself, aren't you?"

"It's Devil's Night. Who else would it be?"

"I told you, the boy toy." No need to tell him her vibe's name was Andrew. He'd just get ideas.

"Bull. Last toy you had was Idiot Luke." His eyes lifted to hers. His brow hiked. "Two months of celibacy, Wild Cat? A fucking crime, with tits like these."

"You don't know that." God, how could he?

He snorted again, so damned cocky she could have nailed him one, had she not been so anxious for him to get to the nailing himself. "Just because you haven't seen me doesn't mean I haven't been around, babe." His hands went to her hips, his fingers curling into the elastic waist of her sweatpants. "Dare I ask what you've got under these?"

"Nothing."

"I wish." He tugged. Pulled her pants over her hips, exposing her in all her pudgy glory. She sweated every inch of extra flesh, willed some trick of the light to make her skinny and attractive. God, she didn't want him pulling away. Not when he'd made her crazy as promised. He got as far as the joint where her leg met her hip before he stopped and lifted impossible-to-read eyes to hers.

"Catharine, you've got to be fucking kidding me."

Chapter Three

Nothing. At first, that's all he saw. Was dimly aware cloth was involved to some degree, but the part that held his attention was the fold of her sex. The lack of anything around it to obstruct his view.

"I told you 'nothing'," she said, and he heard her back starting to rise.

He cut that off quick. Didn't want her prickly, wanted her crazy.

"Shut it, Catharine. Shut up and just let me look for a minute, could you?" How often did a man find his woman waiting in a corset and garters and fucking fishnets and nothing the hell else? How many times could he be lucky enough to stumble across something so erotic? Bloody unexpected, too. Totally out of character. The sweats had been standard Cat but this…This was a dozen wet dreams come true and no one, not even the woman herself, was fucking it up on him.

The line where her lips met held the bulk of his focus, the shine unmistakable even had he missed the distinctive scent of Cat's arousal. Her crease was delicate pink, a sweet contrast to the pale cream of her skin. He'd expected chocolate curls, found only vanilla flesh, and he felt it to the tip of his mushroom head.

No damned room in his jeans. His dick needed serious attention, felt deprived that she'd used that stellar mouth on his finger.

The longer he stared at her swollen lower lips, the more he became aware of the rest of her ensemble. The black garters stretched from corset to thigh high, cutting a dark line over each well-curved leg. The fishnets did amazing things. He didn't know what, just knew he had the impression of miles of dark curves leading away from that hot, wet, pouting crease.

A dozen fantasies rolled into one, bound for his pleasure. Surreal in all the right ways.

She needed to spread more. He needed to see more, every last inch of the hot, slick flesh he planned to use for their mutual pleasure. Didn't have it in him to ask nicely, thought she'd prickle if he asked un-nicely, and decided he'd do best with simple action.

Easy to lay his hands on the webbing over her knees and press down, prodding her to spread lewdly across the couch. One knee rested against the back cushion, the other nearly against the seat. If he could tilt her hips right, he'd have a decent angle to work with, though he suspected releasing her knees would give her a chance to close up on him again.

No way in hell he'd risk that.

"That bad, huh?" she asked. He tried to flick his gaze up to hers in response to the smug, slight mocking in her tone. Couldn't tear himself away from that fascinating slit long enough.

* * * *

The longer he stared, the more she was aware of her nudity. She'd dressed to seduce but hadn't anticipated anyone else seeing it. She'd never dressed like this for anyone, ever. Judging by the non-response coming from Demon Drew, she'd do best to avoid it in future. Much as she'd made her peace with her size — and no one forced to shop in the plus-size section could do less than make tentative peace with their body — she'd never quite embraced it the way the counterculture suggested. She could work the curves to a point but she'd never been comfortable exposing them. Lights-out sex for sure.

Clearly, Drew had no intention of turning off lights. Not with the way he was staring. Didn't even have the balls to look her in the eye, just stared at her bared lower half like it was a train wreck he was rubbernecking.

She blew out a breath in lost irritation. He half-groaned, half-grunted. Who knew what that meant? Probably Neanderthal for "flubby one here, abort mission."

Fucker.

"Hey, champ, none of this was my idea." She drew her knees in, forced his hands out of position as she tried to recover some dignity.

"You're naked," he said and he sounded strange.

"No shit, Sherlock."

Her complexion betrayed her, mottling her precisely as it had her whole life. The flush of embarrassment should clue him in, even if her knees moving hadn't.

The worst of it was that he'd seen her half-naked. Dressed like this, the way she'd always secretly wanted to be. She'd dressed like this and imagined herself sexy, her curves pin-up instead of plump. Somehow, the most appropriate way to spend her first Drew-free Devil's Night involved a little lube, a lot of fantasy, and some quality time with the battery-powered toy that bore his name.

Her little secret, tonight, so she'd let herself go unrestrained. The corset, the garters, the fucking fishnets, all three straight from her if-I-were-a-slut-I'd-wear list. She'd even shaved her dark curls, stripped them with a few minutes' work down and dirty with a handful of cream. Imagined how it might be to have a man there to do it for her, his fingers spreading her lips to coat her with foam, holding her sensitive flesh taut for the blade's edge. Patting her dry with a towel, rubbing her soft with lotion, checking to see that she was as smooth as possible. Playing just because, his fingers oiling her clit.

Even as she'd imagined it, she'd known there was only one man she'd trust to take a razor to such a vital area. Not that he'd ever do it. Not in a million years. Twenty years of friendship and he'd never shown the slightest interest in her quim. Until tonight.

He had to know how wet she was. The corset did well enough to hide her extra pounds but the stretch of material gave away the tightness of her nipples. The pose he'd put her in left her defenseless to his nerve-wracking study. Left her only wiggling her hips to regain a little lost dignity. Too little too late, perhaps, but better than nothing.

She'd wished herself thin before, but never like this. Never wanted to be beautiful more than this moment.

"Christ, Cat," he said again like it was the only thing he could say, and she realized she'd been wrong. The worst wasn't that he'd seen this.

The worst was that he'd seen it and hadn't been inspired by it at all. The sexiest she'd ever been before a man and the only man she'd been seriously interested in couldn't do any more than stare and swear. Definitely not good.

She brought her knees in, tried to close them as best she could. If she couldn't help how she was dressed or how she was built, she could at least control how much more he saw. At first, he simply let his palms rest on her knees as she drew them together, narrowing the angle and twisting so the long, lace-covered length of thunder thigh blocked all but the scent of her arousal.

Just as she thought she was making progress, he snapped out of his daze. Moved his hands down her thighs, his warm, rough palms teasing her as they moved over the open weave of her fishnets to settle where elastic, rubber, and garter clip held the stockings in place.

Then he pushed her legs apart again. Made it clear he wouldn't let her close up on him.

His eyes lifted from her crotch, met hers, and narrowed with something she couldn't name. She'd never seen anything that stark on his face before. Never seen him this intense, this far removed from his ever-ready grin.

"Going somewhere?" he asked, one brow lifting. So sardonic. "Funny, I don't remember saying you could move."

"I don't remember giving you a say."

"The cuffs say different." His thumbs brushed over her inner thighs, so damned close to her slick sex she was sure he'd start spreading her juices over her legs in a second. Oh, God. Wet as she was, angled as she was, no doubt she'd be dripping onto his hands in a minute.

She squeezed her eyes shut, wishing for death.

* * * *

Exquisite. Almost too much too soon, because where the hell did he start on this luscious body? Much as experience said women liked a little foreplay before a guy went headlong into their crotch, he couldn't stop staring. Or thinking. Or picturing how she'd look spread properly for him.

What the hell? She was tied up anyway. Not like she could bolt if she objected. He sniffed again, nearly tasted her on his tongue when he moved in closer to get better acquainted with the sweet musk of her.

He had all the time in the world to get to her fantastic breasts and play in that stellar cleavage. Hadn't really had a plan when he'd slapped the cuffs on her, just assumed he'd go by gut. And if the gut said he should be nose-deep in her juice by now, well, he'd let it play out.

So he did. Moved his hands up her thighs, enjoying the contrast of garter against skin, how the silky softness of Cat made the garters feel rough. If her legs were this damned smooth, her cunt was going to be like satin.

His thumb traced the crease of her kitty, spreading the honey there, painting it so it covered that bare flesh. Fuck. Cat, smooth as a baby's ass, wet as a whore's mouth. Nothing better in the world.

"You're incredible," he said. Found her clit, hard and peeking from its hood, and rolled it under his fingertips until her hips shifted again.

"You're insane."

He flicked her clit. Smiled to himself at the small noise she made in response.

"I'm crazy," he said. Grinned. "So are you."

He sunk a finger into the wet tunnel. Wiggled it, probing, and withdrew to trace the delicate pink petals of flesh that guarded her. She gasped. Swore. Wiggled back like she could make him hit all the right buttons to make her come.

Like he wasn't expecting her to fight him on it. *Silly Wild Cat*, he thought on a wave of fresh affection.

"Drew, please."

"Please what?" He knew. Oh yeah, he knew. She wanted him sliding in, pulling out. Wanted him to fuck her with that finger, let her come on it.

"You like this, don't you, Catharine? My finger in your pussy, opening you up."

"Drew." She'd squeezed her eyes shut, damn it. If she was trying to block him out, he'd get seriously pissed. How could any woman as fucking hot for it be so stubborn?

Screw that. He was stubborn, too. No hiding her response to him, though she was clearly trying to shut him out. Like he was some fucking toy she could ignore.

"I own you, Cat. I could do anything to you right now and you'd just have to take it, wouldn't you?" She moaned. Good girl. "If I want to suck your clit 'til the trick-or-treaters come, there's not a damned thing you can do about it. And if I want to put every finger I've got in this pretty cunt of yours, there's nothing you can do to stop me."

As he said it, the image formed in his mind's eye. His hand, buried to the knuckles in her tight pussy. She didn't feel overly tight at the moment, not with a single finger in her snatch, but from the way she tried to clamp down on that finger, he thought he'd start stretching her fast if he tried. Experience said tight as she was, he'd have a fair bit of stretching to do before he could move beyond fingers, anyway.

"I could put my whole fist up here and you'd let me." For once, it wasn't a question. She grasped at his finger at the thought, proof positive she absolutely would let him put a hand inside her glove. The thought of pushing her limits, teaching her body how far she could go, was irresistible.

The second finger went in easy, a near-perfect fit. As he sunk in to the base, things got almost snug, the smooth wet of her insides clamping down on him. She'd feel like warm, wet heaven on his dick.

Not enough, though, not even when he scissored his fingers inside her. Three went better. Made her noises louder, more needy, as he tucked his middle finger over the other two and sucked hard on her clit.

Her hips bucked. For a heartbeat, he thought she was trying to shake him off her and he lifted his head, worried he'd misread something somewhere. The needy little whimpers said he hadn't, and when her soft, heavy hips lifted up from the couch again to bump his chin with her slick lips, he couldn't help his grin.

He licked at her clit. Lapped at her sex, his tongue parting her lips with his steady, broad sweep.

No trouble at all to lift her thighs and hook her knees over his shoulders, spreading her further and burying his face in fragile, fragrant folds. God Almighty, he never wanted to leave them. She tasted so good. Sweet and salty, like a peach tequila body shot. Went down as smooth, burned just as sweet.

"Damn it, Drew. Make me come."

He stopped then. Lifted his head and stared, waiting. She made him wait, which pissed him off.

"Say it, Wild Cat." She glared like he was being purposely obtuse, which entertained him. Of the two of them, she had obtuse locked. "You know what."

She did her best to gnash her teeth in irritation. "I want you, you bastard," she snarled, too pissed to be placating. "Is that what you wanted to hear? I want you inside me. Now." She rattled her wrists again. He was starting to seriously love that sound as metal clinked against enamel. "For fuck's sakes, uncuff me already. I want to touch you."

He considered her for a second, relishing the flush consuming her, the angry heat flaring off her from every direction.

"What are you waiting for? An engraved invitation?"

He chuckled. "The rest."

"Andrew." Her pissy tone said she'd said all she planned to, so he nodded and ceded her the win, such as it was. Dug into his pocket for the key to her handcuffs, then leaned over her to free one wrist. No point showing her the escape clause, so he drew both her hands away from the table, pulled them to his mouth, and brushed kisses over both sets of knuckles. She relaxed, closing her eyes and smiling victoriously.

Her smile died when he snapped the cuffs back on.

Chapter Four

"You cheated." She glared. He shrugged it off and drew her cuffed hands to his chest to feel her touch. Much as he enjoyed playing with her body — and God, did he love that — he wanted to enjoy her playing with his.

Something she seemed disinclined to do.

"Half an answer, Wild Cat, half a release. Only fair. There were rules, after all." He arched a brow. "Unless you plan to finish that thought for me..?"

"Get stuffed."

"But you'd enjoy it so much more," he said, enchanted by the frustrated lust he saw in the shine of her eyes, the tight set of her lips. Nothing, really, to kiss her again. Not when he was already so close. Her fingers curled when he did. Her palms pressed against his shirt when his tongue slipped into her mouth.

She pushed him back and for a second, he thought he'd misread her. If she was pushing him away, he'd...he didn't even know. Something. No way he'd let her avoid the inevitable, not when she panted for it as hard as he did.

She didn't scramble off the couch, which he'd half-expected. Nor did she wrestle him for the keys.

And if she'd considered reaching for her clothes to cover up on him, well, clearly she'd chosen not to.

Wild Cat wouldn't have stayed half-naked unless she'd intended it, either, which gave him all kinds of hope, but what had him holding his breath was the determined lift of her chin, the defiant set of her shoulders.

Her position changed, went from reclining to kneeling on self-propelled momentum. Pretty tricky stuff for someone on a couch but he wasn't about to complain. Then she bent to crawl across the cushions on her hands and knees, a seductive sway in her big, white hips as she did. God, he could see her ass cheeks tilted provocatively high as she moved.

"Is that what we're here for, Demon Drew? What I'd enjoy?" She slicked her mouth with her tongue as the intent of her words hung over both of them, then pursed her lips into a purely feminine smile as he caught on. "What if I want to see what you'd enjoy?"

"You," he answered too fast. "I'm enjoying you."

"And if I want to enjoy you?"

So much for holding the power in the situation.

* * * *

Strange, how easy this was. Two hours earlier, she wouldn't have thought herself capable of crossing the couch on all fours, half-naked and heading for anyone's crotch, let alone Demon Drew's. Hell, doing this was something out of a hot, vivid fantasy.

It felt like someone else was unbuttoning his dark, heavy jeans. Like someone else's fingers were tugging at his zipper, brushing over the length of cotton covering his erection. She wasn't sure how she managed to do it without passing out as the blood drained from her head but somehow, she did. Must have, because when she touched her tongue to her teeth speculatively and touched him again, she heard him hiss a breath in.

She spread his fly. Considered the sight before her, caught Drew's sharp, male scent and its musky overlay. Knew this single suck would be the most erotic moment of her life.

Which meant bringing out the big guns. The one thing she did very, very well.

She tugged at his pants until he lifted his hips. Pulled them down to his knees then ignored them, far more concerned with the plain white boxer briefs she'd just uncovered than with getting his pants off entirely.

She laid her hand over his crotch and feathered her fingers in a gentle beat against his shaft. He nearly groaned. God knew what that noise he'd just made was, but it wasn't a groan. Not quite. Not yet.

She pulled her fingers away, letting them trail along his length. Kept her eye on the prize despite the temptation to look up when he bit out a curse.

Cat found the flap at his fly and gently, carefully, with just her index fingers, pulled at the sides until a small gap appeared.

Well, hello there. She blew. He shivered.

"Cat," he said, shaky and reaching to pull his shorts down. That's when she looked up. Caught sight of his eyes, dark and unreadable, and the severe intensity on his mouth, the hollows of his cheeks as he sucked in, and shook her head. *Don't touch.*

Rubbed her thumb over the smooth, hard skin she'd bared in a tiny, crazy-making circle. *Mine*.

"You don't want them off?" he asked. Maybe he would have said more, but she pushed the fabric until the head of his cock pushed through the gaping cotton.

Her tongue swirled over his tip as her lips closed over it. He swore again when she sucked in and brought the smoothness of her inner cheeks into contact with his swollen head.

He brushed a stray curl off her forehead and left his hand on her hair in silent approval. Possession.

Then she sucked in harder and pressed down, guiding him into her so he went from cotton to Catharine instantly. His hips twitched off the couch when her nose pressed against his flat abdomen. She felt the crisp mat of fur beneath the cotton and nearly sighed. Might have, but her mouth was full.

She hadn't done this in forever, so when she tilted her head to let all of him in, she had to think about it. Check the angles, as it were. God, he went in so easily considering his bulk and girth. After a moment or two, she couldn't remember anything but the feel of his erection weighing on her tongue and his sharp, musky scent.

He laced his fingers into her hair. Tightened his grip in reflex when she sucked in again.

She hummed until he swore. Slid back until just his head was in her mouth, then closed her hand around his shaft.

Her strokes were erratic. He felt amazing in her hand, like hard, hot brushed silk, the pulsing veins like ribs against her palm. Her tongue swirled over his head as her fingers fluttered.

She snaked one hand up the leg of his boxer briefs. Wished he'd worn boxers so she could get where she was going easier. Thanked God the chain linking her wrists allowed her enough movement to touch him on both sides of his underwear and that he'd worn a pair cut short enough to let her do so with relative ease. If not, she might have had to hit the quick-release latch to get things done right and frankly, she was enjoying this game far too much to wreck it so quickly.

While he had her in cuffs, he assumed he had the upper hand. Not true, but she wasn't about to prove that.

When her fingertips touched the soft, sensitive skin of his sac, she figured she'd done okay, after all. She teased him with her touch, gentle on his testes as her mouth went hard on his cock.

He groaned her name, lost it in a string of profanity that made her feel like a million bucks because when a man swore that much during sex, he was definitely enjoying himself.

He shifted, lifting his hips up to meet her dipping mouth, then wriggling a little so she could cover his balls with her hand inside his shorts.

His fingers tightened in her hair. Were almost tugging, but it felt so damned good she didn't care.

Then she squeezed his sac just hard enough to make him curse again. Her mouth gentled on his cock. The hand on his shaft stilled.

* * * *

She was swallowing him whole. He'd never...God. He'd had women blow him before but this...This was no ordinary blow job.

This was his Wild Cat, doing things to his dick he'd never suspected she knew existed.

Funny, he'd always imagined her to be more of a licker. Truth be told, he'd looked forward to showing her how to use that smart, sexy mouth of hers. Never dreamed she'd know all this from the start.

It would be very wrong of him to thrust now, but God, he wanted to. The urge to grip her by the hair and fuck her mouth like an animal bubbled, nearly irresistible. He flexed once before he caught himself. She moaned at the move, sent the vibration down along his dick and had him swearing again.

Fuck self control. It was overrated, anyway.

He clenched her curls and pumped his hips in once, twice, cautious to catch the potential protests. None. Somehow, he wasn't surprised.

Instead, she sucked harder.

Her teeth grazed against that spot at the base of his head. He saw stars. The hand at his nuts squeezed again, then turned so a finger could smooth over his taint. He shuddered. Not the first time he'd been touched there but definitely the first time he'd been surprised by it.

Though any chick who blew a guy in his shorts obviously had a few tricks up her sleeve, even if she was St. Catharine.

She did it again, sweeping her tongue over his head as she tickled his perineum. He fisted her hair and pumped into that hot, tight throat again, sure this was what waited if he died on the Lord's good side.

"Baby, stop." He tried to stop himself, knew it was unfair to ask her to if he couldn't, but her mouth was incredible, her throat so damned tight, that he nearly lost himself in it. She sucked in response, made his eyes roll. "Baby. Catharine." He clenched his jaw and fought with the urge to spill. "If you don't stop, I'm going to come."

She paused. Looked up at him with those big, beautiful eyes and stared hard, speaking through them because her mouth was full. Of dick. He was buried to the balls in Catharine's sassy mouth and the sight of it blew him away. Better, so much better, than even he'd thought possible.

She sucked again, long and deliberate, her gaze locked on his. "Baby, can I come in your mouth?" His breath was ragged, his words unsteady, but the way she stared made him think it would be okay. "Blink if you want me to come in your mouth."

She blinked. He swallowed. Then she sucked again, the tip of her finger pressing against the tight ring of his anus, and he spilled in that gorgeous mouth.

She swallowed. Her throat tightened and shifted as she did, moving over him like the velvet fist of her pussy would when he got that far. Pleasure roared through him, all of it tied to the woman at his dick swallowing hard.

* * * *

"Jesus, Wild Cat." His eyes were wide. Wild. His breathing was ragged and husky and so sexy, she just about creamed her shorts.

Well, had she still had shorts to cream.

"Surprised?"

"That you're a deep-throater? Uh, yeah. A little."

"We all need our social skills," she said, feeling a little prim, a little slutty, and really confused about how both were possible at once. "You didn't think Luke was with me for my brain, did you?" She laughed. Wished it didn't sound so bitter.

That laugh snapped something in him. He swiveled himself off the couch, pulled his shoes off by stepping on the heel of each respectively, then gyrated his hips to get his jeans to pool at his feet. He stepped out of them, left them abandoned on her living room floor, and stared at her with those wild eyes for a long, inscrutable moment.

"Luke was a moron," he growled.

Then he reached down, grabbed the chain linking her wrists, and hauled her off the couch.

Chapter Five

"*He* was a moron?" She tugged at his grip on her cuffs, determined to get away before this insanity went any further. Not that she got loose, but she tried. "You were the caveman breaking noses in public and *he* was the moron?"

"You know what the fight was about, don't you?"

"You had a moment of drunken idiocy?"

His eyes narrowed. "Not that drunk. I was doing fine until he started gloating."

"Over me?" she scoffed. Luke hadn't been a terrible boyfriend but he'd never been the doting type, either. "He was winding you up because you'd had a dry spell lately."

"Over the blonde he'd picked up while you were in the bathroom."

Something curled in the pit of her stomach, sour and withered. "Sorry?"

"I pointed out that picking up strangers wasn't exactly model boyfriend behavior, but he just wouldn't shut up. I'd spent the whole night drinking myself stupid so I wouldn't haul you into a dark corner, hike your skirt up, and make you scream, and he'd been fishing for someone else."

"So you hit him?"

"Not until he...he said a lot, none of it complementary, and I couldn't let that go."

"What did he say?" She felt ill. Nauseous and faint as she remembered what she'd heard as she'd approached the two of them outside the bar. Two hostile men sniping at each other, one of them running her down. *Drew*, she'd thought, *because how could Luke date her and think that?* But now..."He called me fat, didn't he?"

Drew's lips pressed together into a tight white line, his expression grim and hostile at the memory. "He said a lot I don't want to remember."

"He said a lot you don't want to tell me," she corrected tentatively and earned a tight nod. "I thought it was you."

Which snapped him out of his bad mood and straight to horror. "What? Why?" He blanched as it added up. "That's why you..."

"Kicked you out of my life? Yeah." She ached to go back and set things right, to erase the past two months of misery. God, she'd missed him. "I'm sorry."

He melted against her, collapsing in to fold her in the warm, broad shelter of his body, and the heat built again, an insistent urge to touch him.

For a long moment, they were silent, letting the mistakes of the past settle. Difficult to swallow the bitter regret at her own behavior, but she did all the same because she'd hurt him, hurt them both, and she had to make it right somehow.

Then he lifted his head and his mouth pulled into a wicked grin.

"How sorry?"

She considered the question, half in payback for the untenable way he'd stripped her bare for *conversation*, half to catch her breath before the next assault. If she took a minute longer than strictly necessary to watch that wicked sparkle in his gorgeous eyes, well, surely she'd earned that much.

"You should really uncuff me now. It'll be really awkward wall sex if you don't."

Which apparently set off his caveman tendencies.

His mouth was all over hers. Fit like it belonged there and roped her in like he was feeding her Spanish Fly through osmosis. He tore at the corset awkwardly, like he hadn't taken off a million corsets before. Bless him, the boy was learning.

"You love me?" he asked, but it was so harsh and choppy and his hands were so fiendishly fumbling towards ecstasy that it took a bit for her to comprehend. Conversation and consummation definitely didn't mix. Notes, she supposed, for next time.

She hauled his mouth back to hers and nodded as she kissed him, not caring at all that they were bumping each other like post-prom first-timers setting records before curfew.

Damn his eyes, he pulled back again. Frowned but not quite, some expression too complex for her quick-scan to grasp. Brutal, that he had this much self-control. She was in fishnets and half a corset and he…he was still mostly dressed. Pantless, sure, but given where the orgasms had settled tonight, it seemed unfair that she'd bared so much and come so little.

"I swear to God, you shouldn't still be dressed," she muttered, pulling at his shirt. *Off off off.* He went passive enough to let her tug it over his head, leaning forward and rolling his shoulders when it snagged.

"Cat," he said. "Catharine."

The correction had her hands stopping on his chest and looking up, annoyed. "Oh my God, how are you this slow?"

He had to grab her wrists to hold her still. Felt the cuffs and nearly fucking laughed, except that it wasn't actually funny. She was in cuffs, he was in knots, and neither of them were anywhere close to her bedroom.

"Do you love me?" he repeated, forcing the words out so slow, they ceased to be a question.

"Since the damned milk crates."

Then she attacked him again.

* * * *

It twigged as he hit the bed, hauled down by one very determined Wild Cat. Not graceful or slick or any of the things he would have expected, but given the cuffs limiting her movement and the ferocity that seemed to be driving her, not really beyond reason, either.

She leaned in over him, her hands sliding up his thighs like she enjoyed the coarse hair and hard muscle, her mouth so close to his cock, he had visions of happy tears in his future if she moved just a little. He knew, just *knew* he was wearing the dopiest smile ever. Didn't actually care, because it was Wild Cat and she'd loved him since forever, and remembering the way that luscious mouth said "milk crates" made him want to dance naked in victory.

Apparently, love need not mean dignity.

"What, it never came up?"

"If it helps any, I only wanted your body from about fifteen on," she offered. His brows went up at the thought of a damned decade of hot, sweaty nights he could have had. Jesus. They could be married with kids by now. They could have avoided the entire ugly Luke incident. *Maybe he should have been on the short bus.*

"Fifteen?"

She nodded again. Sweet of her, but dangerous given the rough positioning of her head in proximity to his...*Focus.* "Yeah." She licked her lips and made him think of a dozen naughty variations on the theme he'd like to try just as soon as they'd gotten this weird confessions-of-mutual-stupidity out of the way. "Before then, I just used to write Mrs. Drew Benedict on my notebooks."

Holy shit. Holy...He'd planned a down-on-one-knee deal, possibly around Christmas when he'd hopefully have convinced her they were perfectly matched, but sometimes, you just had to chuck the plan.

* * * *

"So we're all set then." He grinned.

Not naked. Why weren't they naked? They should be. Were supposed to be, she was sure. There'd been tearing at clothes and a great deal more foreplay than she'd had with any of her dubious-decision partners. Hell, there'd even been emotions and a whole "I love you" vibe going on.

He was Drew Benedict, the hottest thing on legs in her universe, and he loved her. On her bed, half-dressed, hung like a horse and hard as amour, and *he loved her*.

Oh, they should *totally* be naked now.

Only he was grinning at her, watching her expectantly, and she wanted to scream with frustration at the O he'd promised with his wicked mouth and never quite delivered on.

"All set for what?" she asked, low and demonic. Come-suppression apparently made her sound like something from *The Shining*.

"Mrs. Drew Benedict, huh?" He half-leered, half-peered. "Still got any ambitions in that direction?"

"What?" Stupid, how that was the only word she could remember.

"You love me." Damn him, he sounded wistful. If he went dreamy on her now, she wasn't even waiting to get him naked anymore, just sinking onto that lovely, massive erection of his and rocking until she went Vesuvius on him.

"You're too damned dressed and I'm still not getting any," she said, then sighed at the tender look on his face. "You really don't care I'm...the eff word?"

"You're not," he corrected. "You're full and ripe and lush and I've got this crazy idea that I want to spend the rest of my life getting lost in your sweet, sweet ass. Even if you were the eff word, it wouldn't matter." He reached down. Took hold of her hand and tugged her on top of him. Didn't let on at all if it winded him when she fell, just smiled beautifully and held her close. "You're my girl, Wild Cat. Always have been, even when you were dating morons and I was breaking noses to uphold your honor. I'm a nut without you. Can't even imagine spending a Devil's Night with anyone else, ever, and frankly, I don't want to have to."

She blinked fast and fluttery. "That was...perfect." She snaked her hands free, curled them around his throat to pull him in for a languid kiss to prove her point. "Yes." He beamed. "Now will there be sex?"

* * * *

He rolled them over in a heartbeat. Held her wrist over her head with one hand and fought with the last of her corset hooks with the other, tasting her as he went. Smacked his lips after an experimental lick of the curve of her breast, then settled in to worship properly, losing himself in the soft line of cleavage, testing the weight and give of her fleshy swells in his big, broad hands.

Breasts this good really should be a religion.

She whimpered when his tongue flicked over the stiff, sensitive nub of her nipple. If he called her on it, she'd deny it, of course, but he knew a whimper when he heard one, so he held the thrill of accomplishment it sparked to himself and did it again to prove his point. Wondered when he'd learn to play her body properly, where to touch, how to taste, to make her beg.

The taste of her caught him off-guard. Peaches and salt and something he didn't want to define, so he just called it Cat and moved the hell on. In his player days, he'd have gone straight for home plate because by this point, foreplay was extraneous, but it was Cat and damn it, he wanted more of the whimpering. Well, he wanted things he wasn't sure the human body could *do* without chiropractic assistance later, but he'd settle for the whimpering.

So he set about exploring her properly, and if it took his tongue to do it, so be it.

* * * *

Drew could talk her to orgasm. Hell, he could probably *look* her to orgasm, the way he was going, but between his wicked tongue and his knowing hands, she melted. Though how she'd ever tell anyone how he'd proposed without turning into a human cranberry was beyond her.

As was the rest of his game plan, because he avoided the standard erogenous zones and mapped out new ones. Licked and kissed and sucked and teased *everywhere* but where she was dying for his touch, and the more she protested, the more he evaded. Like it was funny that she'd gone pliant and needy.

Someday, she swore, she'd cuff him up and return the favor.

"I won't beg," she said, gritting her teeth and squirming against him to ease some of the ache between her thighs. He snickered and did something unholy to her navel. Oh, God, she was *panting*.

He looked up long enough to say "Sure you will," and wink, then reapplied himself to his task until he proved it. He lifted off her, which seemed like progress, so she spread her legs and clenched her quim in anticipation of his thick erection sliding inside. Found herself flipped onto her stomach instead and felt his tongue drag along her spine, his hands kneading her ass. She winced at the dough references floating through her mind, then gasped when he bit. Begged again.

"Andrew, now. Please, God, now."

He chuckled again, laved his tongue over the bite, then moved on to do it again on the other side.

"Every inch of you," he said. "I own you, Wild Cat. Get used to it."

Then his fingers stroked the crease of her pussy lips gently, tracing the slick he'd created, spreading it like lotion, his touch reverent. Gentle. Loving, and when she spread for him, it was her way of loving him back. Submission didn't come easily but if that's what he wanted, she'd try.

He fucked her first on his fingers, curling them to stroke her G-spot with feather-light touches, his thumb angled to hit her clit while his mouth claimed her back, her spine, her sides, her hips, whatever he found in his rambling, twisting exploration. When he turned her over again, she didn't say a word, just reclined and let him have whatever access he wanted.

Before he touched her wet, aching sex again, he pressed soft kisses to her inner thighs, marking his passage. She clawed at the headboard, scrambling for purchase before his tongue made contact and she forgot to breathe.

She barely managed.

Whimpered again when his tongue dragged over the crease of her lower lips, teasing and toying like an intimate, mischievous kiss.

Drew marked his possession there, too, with quick light laps and broad sweeps that mapped her labia. Quick flicks of blunted tongue tip working over her clit, dipping into her creamy quim.

Cat had her fingers twined in his hair, fisting it impatiently before she was even aware she'd let go of the headboard. He stopped what he was doing and looked up at her, face shiny with her juice.

"Hands over your head, Catharine. Don't rush this."

"Then stop playing with me."

One brow hiked high on his forehead. "You're not enjoying this?"

"I want you inside me," she said. "I want to feel you come."

He half laughed, half choked. "Well, when you put it that way..."

Then he was over her properly, his hard body covering hers, rubbing everywhere as he positioned his erection at her entrance. Pushed in a little and hissed out a breath between gritted teeth. She hooked her legs over his, stroked his calves with her feet, his thighs with hers, desperate to touch him any way she could. With her hands out of commission, that was harder than she wanted, but there wasn't much she wouldn't do for Drew Benedict, so she kissed whatever she could reach of his face, lips, chin, cheek, nose, anything just to touch.

Tasted herself when she did and didn't mind.

He slid in slowly, stretching her, stroking her sides, kissing her throat. Which moved him out of kissing range, but with his cock inside her at long bloody last, she could live with it. Another perfect fit, which didn't surprise her in the slightest. She gnawed her lip as he pushed deeper, held his gaze when it met hers so he'd see everything she couldn't say. How wonderful he felt, how much she wanted him in deep forever. She didn't cry over sex, not after, not during, but if he stayed this sweet, she thought she just might. Because this…this wasn't just sex.

His hands gripped her waist—had she had one—and he flexed his hips, a single hard thrust that filled her. She moved into him, urged him on, and groaned when he withdrew. Groaned again at his next thrust.

"Okay?"

She nodded. "More."

"That I can do."

He switched angles, altered pace, building the pleasure but never enough to satisfy completely.

"Clit tease," she whispered, which had him reaching down to circle his thumb over her button. She ground in and tried to ride the sensation to release, clamping down on his cock to hold him in, undulating to follow him when he pulled back.

"You love it."

"I'd love it more if you'd stop playing. Fuck me, Drew. Hard. Please?" Heat crept up her face at the directness, so at odds with the mood he'd set, but he'd drawn it out too much, played too long.

"Is that a complaint?" He hiked a brow. Kissed her, then grinned. Which bloody did it. She rolled them both and rode him, setting the pace she wanted. Took him deeper this way and did it just as hard and fast as she needed. When she leaned over him, hands planted on the headboard to hold herself steady, the head of his cock rubbed against the flexing walls of her pussy, bumping and teasing enough to make her bear down on him to spread the stretch. "You squirt when you come, Wild Cat?"

Her breath hitched. She sped up, chased the orgasm tantalizingly out of reach, and sought his smart mouth to shut him up. Her breasts swayed with each move, the hardened tips rubbing lightly against his chest, sending shivers straight to her sex that quivered her inner muscles. She'd never felt this connected, this aware of her own body and its potential for pleasure, but it still wasn't enough. God, how frustrating. Surely if they hadn't stopped for…if he'd just…

"If you lean back, we'll find out," he said, the wildness in his eyes at odds with the calm tone.

"Son of a…" Her breath ran out before she could finish. "Drew…" Even to her own ears, his name sounded needy. Half prayer, half profanity. Her body strained for release, her pulse a rush in her ears. He snapped his hips, drove in hard and deep, unrelenting until she matched his pace. Any second, she'd come. She just knew it. Could hardly stand the wait.

As it built to a peak, he slowed. Winked when she swore.

"I like you this way." His smile was entirely too smug, so she grazed that sensitive spot beneath his ear with her teeth until he swore, too. "Hellcat."

Damp heat hung in the air, coated them both with the sheen of musk and sex and sweat. Everywhere they touched, they did with delicious friction, dragging animal sounds from her throat. "Bloody tease."

"Patient," he corrected. Rolled her beneath him again, guided her legs up around his hips, and filled her again, his cock rubbing over her g-spot as he did. She shuddered. Panted. "There we go."

Oh, God. She was going crazy and he sounded chipper. The cuffs might limit what she did with her hands but she could grip his hair just fine, so she did. "Fuck. Me. Now."

Then he was, his thrusts at perfect rhythm for her clenching sex, triggering her.

"Come for me, sweetheart."

She did. Broke with the force of it, pulse skittering, breath erratic, vision graying as her orgasm pushed through the tension of her body to swamp her in burning, pulsing pleasure.

He nuzzled her, pressed light kisses and let her ride out the sensation. Eyed her speculatively while she tremored with light aftershocks.

"Are you a multiples girl?"

She rolled her eyes. Snuggled in to him.

"I love you," she said, and this time, he laughed. Did the only thing possible under the circumstances…

He unlocked her cuffs.

Daringly Delicious
Leigh Ellwood

Also by Leigh Ellwood

In the Dareville series…

Truth or Dare
Dare Me
Daring Young Man
Double Dare
A Winter's Dare

Also available…

Jilted
Surveillance
Why, Why, Zed?

and many more…

Author's Note

Dearest friends of Dareville,

I thank you for taking the time to read this latest adventure of the small town with big romance. Since publishing *Truth or Dare* in 2004 with Phaze, I hadn't expected to expand the series as far as I have, and I'm far from finished! I hope you'll stay a while and enjoy the scenery.

With regards to *Daringly Delicious'* place in the Dareville chronology, I will note that this short—while a hot story on its own—works as a companion piece to the upcoming *Dare to Dream* and the forthcoming *Dare Devils*, as all three stories will run in a concurrent timeline with another coming story, *Daring Red*. Therefore, the chronological order of the series will eventually read thus:

Truth or Dare
Dare Me
Double Dare
Daring Young Man
Dare to Dream (not yet published)
Daringly Delicious
Dare Devils (not yet published)

MORESCA, WINSTON, ELLWOOD, BLISSE

Daring Red (not yet published)
A Winter's Dare

But there's always room in town for more.

Stay daring,

Leigh

Chapter One

"Oh. My. Fuck. Ing. *God!*"

That was what Tish heard, anyway. Despite the hopefully positive body language Lauren Marbury exhibited—the dreamy smile, the raised eyebrows—Tish remained apprehensive. Perhaps if Lauren had waited until after swallowing the truffle to give her critique, she might have better interpreted the words.

Lauren appeared to have just finished off the one when she reached into the plastic container for another bonbon. The dark chocolate shell crackled between her teeth, and a diamond-shaped sliver broke away and landed on the heel of Lauren's hand as she pulled it away. Tish could tell by the white pinwheel design piped around the truffle that Lauren had selected the chocolate key lime flavor—her signature concoction.

Appreciative moaning followed Lauren's devouring of the second candy, and the woman licked the smeared chocolate from her fingers and palm. This Tish took as a good sign and she relaxed in the molded retro chair opposite Lauren's. They sat in the little café dining area of Jake's Organic—it was early and the store would open in thirty minutes. All around them workers in dark green shirts and long khaki pants bustled up and down aisles of shelves and the bank of registers, preparing for the new business day. Tish let the activity distract her momentarily as she remembered her days of punching a clock to make money on somebody else's time. No more.

Thank the angels and saints she had the talent and drive to go into business for herself. She could wear any color she chose — a fortunate thing, since only so many shades complimented her large frame.

"Good *night*, lady!" Lauren sounded out of breath. "I think I need a cigarette now." She patted her breastbone, stifling a burp, and brushed her hand against Tish's with a laugh. Tish realized she must have looked surprised at the comment, and Lauren's gesture served to assure her. Clients and potential clients often praised her work, but never before compared it to sex.

Like I'd know, she thought with some sarcasm. She pulled the hem of her short skirt over her chubby legs. Her "lucky" outfit — worn only to important meetings — began to feel a bit tight on her. Seeing how far back the hem of her skirt pulled when she first sat shocked Tish, and she realized she needed to stop eating so many of her culinary mistakes.

"I take it you like the samples," she finally addressed Lauren's enthusiasm.

"I *adore* the samples. I've tasted so many dry and tasteless cakes and goodies this week, I swear I was spitting out sand afterward. But this," Lauren gestured to the sample tier of buttercream enrobed chocolate cake — crumbs sprinkling the wedge space where a piece had been cut — and the box of truffles, "is absolutely scrumptious."

"Thank you," Tish said.

"And you don't have any exclusive agreements to supply cakes anywhere else?"

"No. I only just started with the cakes." The swish of the nearby automatic sliding doors momentarily distracted Tish. The gorgeous hunk of man entering the store continued to hold her attention.

"The truffles are distributed all over Hampton Roads...and the Internet," she managed before her voice died. Did she have a website? She couldn't remember anymore. Her own name turned fuzzy and lost in the powerful aura given off by the sexy, dark man scanning the breadth of the store for assistance. He stood tall in a form-fitting white t-shirt that nicely set off his tanned arms, and black slacks helped display a nicely-rounded ass. Muscles twitched and cords in his neck tightened—he appeared anxious.

Pity. A more attractive, confident Tish might have extracted herself from the business meeting to offer the handsome stranger the opportunity to relieve that tension. She could guide him to the baking aisle, and select any of a wide variety of oils for a sensual massage.

I can knead dough, but I need a man.

She wished she could cross her legs to stop the rising throb in her pussy. She reached for a truffle and set it before her. No, she would not satisfy lust again with a fattening substitute.

All the while she listened to the store manager babble about her new wedding and special occasions registry, and how Jake's had contracted with local florists and photographers, yada yada, but nothing was exclusive.

"Definitely, we'll want to carry your truffles in the café." Lauren twisted in her chair and gestured to the dessert display case. Hands fluttered, fingers snapped. Tish saw Lauren as a performance in excited body semaphore. "But an exclusive agreement to sell your wedding cakes through us would be wonderful," Lauren continued. "We'd make it worth your while. We're getting so many queries now, and nobody wants to go all the way to the beach for a cake. Other types of cake that you make, you could sell here and elsewhere..."

"Sure." She glanced back to face Lauren, then another quick peek. He was gone in that split-second.

Good.

A more distracted Tish might have eaten the truffle, the box, then signed away her secret recipes if Lauren had slipped a blank paper under her hand to sign. The truffles alone provided good income for her, and Tish didn't want cake baking to cut into that.

"I don't bake many cakes as it is," she told Lauren. "I should be able to handle what comes through the store."

Cake eating, on the other hand, could prove to be disastrous if the wedding business boomed. Tish envisioned her kitchen sink, piled high with chocolate-smudged forks and plates, herself slumped to the floor in a diabetic coma, and shuddered.

"Excellent!" Lauren clasped her hands. "I have to tell you, the timing couldn't be more perfect. Our first wedding is scheduled in a month and we have everything done but the cake—"

"A month?" Tish exclaimed. Nothing like the cold hand of reality to kill an amorous mood. At best she figured she had a month to negotiate contracts and establish herself with the store before she actually had to deliver something. "You don't waste time, do you?"

Lauren seemed less concerned with the looming deadline. She scratched rapidly into a checkbook with a ball-point pen. "It's not a huge affair, about seventy-five people at best, all local. We don't have anything after that until June, so there's time to recover." She ripped away the check and handed it to Tish. "How's this for an advance?"

Tish tried not to let her eyes widen and bug out of her head like that of a cartoon character. "Thanks for the vote of confidence," she said, tucking the check into her purse. "I trust the bride and groom have a design and flavor in mind?"

"The bride and groom would be happy with a sheet cake from Winn-Dixie and a punch bowl full of Sprite and sherbet," Lauren rolled her eyes. "They left everything to me, to their credit. They'd be ordering pizzas for the reception otherwise. Here you go. I even made a sketch of what the cake should look like. Everything you need to know is right there."

"Not a bad idea. Delivery in thirty minutes or your wedding's free." Tish took the detailed cake specifications and the purchase order for truffles. Assuming the cake would be a probationary assignment, she would not expect a contract until after she finished the job.

But Lauren surprised her again. "Jake has the contracts in the office. If you can wait a few minutes, we'll print one out for you. There he is!"

Lauren leaped from her chair, gesticulating wildly once again. Tish shifted in her chair for a better view of the approaching store owner and froze at the sight of her mystery man close on his heels. She remained still, but her body responded against her will—her nipples poked against her thin top, and a warmth shot down her spine to her pussy, where it pooled into lava.

"Here she is," Jake Marbury gestured to Lauren, and the man extended his hand over the table. Of course, he didn't give fat Tish Richmond a cursory glance.

"I'm Vinnie Petrocelli," he greeted her. "My Uncle Dom sent me to drop these off." He spoke softly, with an accent nowhere near Virginian. If Tish had to guess...New York, from some ethnic borough where children played in the geyser streams of open fire hydrants in the sticky summertime. He had the look of somebody new to small town Dareville, and as he bent over the table to give Lauren a large manila envelope Tish caught scents of bold aftershave and earthy tobacco.

Smoker, eh? Not that it mattered. Men like that simply didn't ask her out to dinner, but only to move out of the way so they can pass and talk to the skinny blonde walking three paces ahead.

"Excellent!" It appeared to be a catchphrase for Lauren. "And since we're all going to be working together, I'd like you both to meet Tish Richmond. She made these incredible truffles. You have to try them."

Niceties and handshakes exchanged, Tish held Vinnie's gaze and palm for only a few seconds, yet it felt years of acquaintance passed between them. The energy vibrating through his body into hers ignited a delicious sensation that tickled her insides. Would it be possible to orgasm from an indirect touch? Tish wasn't about to humiliate herself by becoming the guinea pig for that experiment. She broke contact quickly and rose.

"I hope I'm not being too rude," she focused on Lauren to stay calm, "but I have another delivery to make. You can just e-mail me the agreement and I'll bring it back. My address is on the card."

She managed a clean getaway, which Jake didn't seem to mind since he insisted Lauren speak with Vinnie about his papers. As she retreated, Tish wondered about him, and how he and "Uncle Dom" figured into Lauren's wedding planner business.

Behind her, Lauren implored both men again to sample Tish's bon-bons. "Tell me this isn't the most delicious thing you've ever tasted," she challenged.

Curiosity got the better of Tish. Turning back, she caught Vinnie licking chocolate from his fingers and lips. Another crescent shaped bite of truffle cradled in the other hand. "It's pretty damn close," he said, nodding with a smile.

He looked right at Tish as he said it.

Chapter Two

Vinnie turned the Caddy into the lot of Big Apple Limos, reaching over to still the sliding pastry box resting on the passenger seat. After dropping off his uncle's contracts at the grocery store, Lauren Marbury plied him with an assortment of treats to take back to work. Vinnie wasn't sure how the other drivers would like organic cookies and tarts, but he knew his cousin's wife, Lupe, would appreciate the fruit salad Lauren picked especially for her.

He parked the car in his uncle's spot by the back door, then gently took the smaller of the two boxes given him from the center console in hand. These, he had no intention of sharing.

"*Buenos tardes,*" he greeted Lupe's bent form. She was filing papers behind the main reception desk, displaying a perfectly heart-shaped bottom in a red tailored skirt. His cousin Robbie was a lucky man to have such a lovely wife — kind and generous enough to help him with his Spanish. "*¿Donde esta mi tio?*"

A lusty chuckle sounded from the file cabinet, and Vinnie quickly realized his error. Right words, perhaps, but definitely the wrong girl. Vinnie stepped back as the figure stretched upward to reveal herself not as Lupe, but her younger, perpetually horny sister, Lola.

She turned toward him, thrusting low to flash her caramel-colored bosom, encased in a sinfully cut blouse. "*Dias*," she corrected him, "it's a bit too early for *tardes*, and way too early for *noches*."

"I knew that," he said, annoyed and uncomfortable. "Where's Lupe? Today's not her day off."

Lola shrugged. "We traded places today. Lu and Robbie have concert tickets tonight. Easier for them to stay out there," she said, "out there" referring to the Virginia Beach office of Big Apple.

"Convenient." For all parties involved, anyway. Vinnie knew Robbie could work out of the satellite office, and here Lola could tap into a different pool of drivers for her sexual exploits, if she hadn't already.

It also meant Robbie's office would be vacant for the day, allowing him some privacy until Uncle Dom needed him. But first...

"Uncle Dom around?" he asked in English this time, putting more distance between them as Lola sashayed closer. "I need to ask him something."

"In his office, on the phone." Lola crooked her head to her right, stretching her long, slender neck. "You know, if you want to brush up on your Spanish some more I can give you some private lessons. I speak it as well as Lupe." Her hand came up to her throat in a seductive gesture, sliding down to the top of one mound and holding still. "It's been pretty slow today. I could teach you a few, ah, phrases."

Positions, too, no doubt. Vinnie shook his head. "I'm sure it'll pick up soon. Better stick by the phones." With that, Vinnie made a beeline for Dom's office. The idea of being another "noche" on Lola's bedpost held no appeal. The girl was pretty, surely fun to be around, but she lacked the substance Vinnie looked for in a woman.

He set the large pastry box on Dom's desk as his uncle finished his call, then took the smaller box for himself. This substance would have to suffice for now.

"Compliments of Jake's Organic," he told his uncle, who already had a treat in hand once the phone call was disconnected. "We're all set. Our first wedding gig with them is next month."

"*Bene*," Dom smiled through the first bite, and waved Vinnie to sit. "I just landed a deal with Plaza Guadalajara at the beach. We are now their official comp shuttle on Friday nights starting this week. All three locations."

"Damn, that's a sweet deal!" Vinnie hadn't been in Virginia long—only a few months following his uncle's job offer—but it didn't take him long to find the local hot spots. The popular Mexican restaurant chain, particularly the Oceanfront location, was always packed. For certain, their drivers would fight to work those shifts, and reap all the tips from weekend revelers. "How'd you swing that?"

Dom shrugged modestly, but Vinnie knew well of his uncle's business savvy. "The guys they have now, not so reliable. They're ready for a change. Plus, it helped that they were impressed that Cal Briscoe is a regular client."

Vinnie laughed. The Dareville musician and his band had a large following in the area. A local appearance usually meant a capacity audience.

"And with all the girls' night out business they get, they'll need some good-looking drivers to take them home, eh?" Dom winked.

"Don't tell Lola."

Dom scoffed, and Vinnie nodded. Lola might welcome the audience, or extra participants, for all they knew.

"So," Dom brought out a note pad. "Which shifts do you want? I'm guessing the later you work, the luckier you might get."

"Actually…" Vinnie toyed with the small box on his lap. "I think I got lucky today. I met the lady who's gonna make the wedding cakes for Jake's store."

Dom arched an eyebrow and smirked.

"You know how you talk about meeting Aunt Ginny for the first time? How you knew right away she was the one? I think that happened to me with this girl." Vinnie's smile quickly fell. "But I was too struck dumb to say anything."

"Aw, hey." Dom leaned back in his chair. Hinges squealed their protest, making Vinnie wince. "No need to feel down about it. You say she's working for the Marburys' store? Stands to reason your paths will cross again soon. By then I'm sure you'll have the courage to speak up," Dom said. "In the meantime, I'll schedule you for their first wedding, how's that sound?"

"Don't think I can wait a month," Vinnie grumbled.

"Well, you know she's not going anywhere before then, and you might find you need a month to work up the nerve. Took me that long to say hello to your Aunt Ginny and keep it to two syllables." Dom chuckled. "Lucky for me, I was too cute for her to resist."

Vinnie shook his head. His uncle carried himself so confidently, it seemed difficult to imagine him tongue-tied in front of a lady, especially given the way he wooed the various women of Dareville who came seeking his business.

"Maybe you're right," Vinnie said, standing. "I gotta make a call. I'll be in Robbie's office for a bit, then I'll be in the garage." The one advantage to having a chauffeur who could also service vehicles — one less check for Dom to write. Vinnie imagined his uncle appreciated the extra work he put in at Big Apple, otherwise Vinnie wouldn't have so much free rein about the place.

Changing oil, however, could wait. As he left his uncle's office he noticed Lola exiting toward the garage area, one of the younger drivers in tow. If she were smart, she set the phone system to have calls routed there while she helped test the shocks of whatever limo they would use for their *buenos dias*.

He had half a mind to squeal on her, but Dom surprised him. "Do what you gotta do," he said, "I'll handle our little back seat driver."

Vinnie looked back, surprised by the look on his uncle's face. "You sure?"

Dom winked.

* * * *

Locking the door, Vinnie settled himself on Robbie's chair and proped his feet on a clear spot on the desk. Opening the box revealed two perfect, petite truffles Lauren Marbury had given him. *Tell me this isn't the most delicious thing you've ever tasted*, she'd challenged, and he had to be truthful. The dark chocolate raspberry confection he'd sampled at the store exploded in a rich, flavorful symphony that certainly spoiled him on store-bought snacks. His favorite peanut butter cup treat just wasn't going to do it for him anymore.

That was when Lauren gifted him with the peanut butter truffles. "One milk, one dark," she'd said. "It's all good." He'd soon find out, he mused, noting the tan piping shaped like a peanut on each shell. If these were half as delicious as the other one…

…and half as yummy as the woman who made them…

He closed his eyes to conjure an image of the lovely Tish Richmond, reviewing every step of her shapely retreat from the store. He couldn't help his full-blooded Sicilian nature—he liked his women thick, and had more than his fill of plastic Manhattan toothpicks over the years. When Uncle Dom offered him work in Dareville he hoped for a change in scenery—in more ways than one—and had been ready to give up when he went to Jake's Organic to drop off the contracts for his uncle.

His teeth sank deeply into the first truffle. The melting shell slid between his heated, pinched fingers just as the creamy peanut butter spread over his tongue and upper palate. He savored the salty tang, coupled with a hint of vanilla, and wondered what it would be like to delve his tongue into Miss Richmond's sticky sweet core for a different taste sensation.

Damn. Never before had eating candy made him hard. He palmed the growing bulge in his pants, unable to recall the last time a woman had excited him so. He ached with the fantasy of Tish Richmond, naked but for a skimpy apron, bending over a mixing bowl so that her ample bottom was raised toward his waiting cock. He wouldn't be able to disappear inside her fast enough.

Nimbly his fingers found the zipper of his fly and eased away the fabric so he could slip inside the flap of his briefs for his cock. The chocolate on his fingers provided suitable lubrication, and he wrapped himself with his fist, pumping up and down in short bursts.

Yes, first he'd grab those swollen cheeks in both hands, kneading them as she might with pastry dough. Then he'd kneel low before her, split them wide after a generous kiss to the base of her spine, then tease her anus with his tongue, all the while trailing one hand underneath to finger her clit. After she came he'd go for the kill, and plunge his cock into her warm, wet depths.

Right now, his cock felt close to release. With the truffle still in his other hand, he flicked at the dense gooey center, pretending to do the same to her pussy. His balls tightened and tingled below his grasp. Willing his orgasm forward, one-two-three last jerks on his rod set forth a stream of come he turned upward so as not to splatter Robbie's desk.

"Criminy," he muttered, opening his eyes to inspect the damage. Brown and white stains clumped his t-shirt, but luckily he kept spares in his locker at work. It would mean having to pass Lola in a shirtless state and perhaps arouse her attention, but the thought didn't bother him. Likely another driver had her distracted.

The only thing that concerned Vinnie now was how to end up shirtless, and more, with Tish Richmond.

Chapter Three

"Hello?"

The receptionist's desk stood unoccupied, yet the faint strains of an oldies rock station wafted throughout the lobby. An open door behind the desk indicated a copy machine ran, given by the gentle whirring sound and sideways shadows cast on the wall within. Tish dipped her head for a closer look, but couldn't see anybody.

"Hello?" She tried a bolder greeting.

"One moment, *por favor*," called an accented, feminine voice. "Have a seat, I'll be right out."

Tish obliged, setting her bag on a coffee table littered with expired magazines. She flipped idly through a *People*, feeling her self esteem drop with every picture of a size-two starlet in a barely there gown, when she heard a second voice snap from the copy room.

They spoke rapidly in a foreign tongue, not Spanish. Tish knew enough from college to converse casually, and this was close. More shadows flickered, and the voices grew louder as two beautiful women who could have stepped out of the magazine Tish held came into view.

The taller of the two, dressed conservatively in a melon colored pantsuit, as opposed to the other's cut off jeans and a tank top, smiled graciously at Tish. She ended the other girl's chatter with a terse glance. "Sorry to keep you waiting," she told Tish. "How may I help you today?"

"Uh, hi." Tish rose, taking the bag with her to the desk. Seeing the more casual of the pair eying her with some amusement unnerved her. Tish immediately felt thick and uncomfortable in her plus size jeans and kimono style top. "I am Tish Richmond with Tish's Riches. Lauren Marbury suggested I come here today and talk to..."

She plucked a sticky note from the bag. "Dominic Petrocelli."

"Mr. Petrocelli is out this morning, but maybe I can help. I'm Lupe. Lola, please!" She admonished the other woman, who now boldly leaned close to Tish to see into the bag.

"What?" Lola snapped, sounding as though she were in the right with her snooping. "I just want to see."

"It's okay. I wanted to drop these off for Mr. Petrocelli, and anybody else interested." Tish brought out the boxes of assorted truffles, then handed Lupe her card. "Since I signed with Jake's Organic yesterday to make their wedding cakes, Lauren suggested I come here as well to offer my services."

"Certainly." Lupe filed the card in a small box. "We offer various packages where people can order champagne or roses for their limo. Gourmet chocolate will go over big."

Tish bit her lip, tempted to laugh at the other woman's zealous reaction to her offering. The Latina beauty snatched the top tier and made for a side door, babbling something before making her exit. Lupe let out an exhausted breath when the door slammed shut.

"Please forgive my sister," she pleaded with Tish. "Lola can be a bit, ah, oblivious at times. Usually on days ending in Y."

"She's very pretty," Tish said, a spontaneous remark.

"So are you."

Lupe's response caught Tish off guard. Her head turned away from the door Lola passed through to where Lupe had opened a box. "And this," Lupe added, holding a half-eaten truffle, "is quite possibly the best piece of candy I've ever eaten."

"Thank you." Tish noted the teeth indentations in the chocolate shell, and the concave curve left in the smooth, orange nougat. A perfect bite with perfect teeth, the candy pinched between elegantly painted nails. Thinner women ate sexier than she did, too. How could she stand a chance?

Lupe popped the remainder in her mouth, licking a stray sugar speck from her lower lip. "And you made these yourself?"

"Every last one. I ship them everywhere, you can order online. I'll also have them at both of Jake's Organics stores, too," Tish said.

"Really? You ship to Brazil?"

Tish thought a moment, working out the postage in her head. "Well, I haven't before, but I can. Just to warn you, though, holidays get busy so you should order early." She paused, then, "That's where you're from? I know that wasn't Spanish you were speaking earlier. So it was Portuguese?"

Lupe nodded. "Lola and I are from Rio, but I also speak Spanish and a few other languages. Spanish is more in demand here, so I tend to speak it more often."

The other woman's smile was friendly and easy. Tish relaxed, feeling more comfortable with this beautiful woman. How nice to be so confident—if only she could bottle some of Lupe's exuberance and beauty for herself. "Too bad one of them isn't French. I could use a translator for my website."

"Ah, *mais oui*," Lupe exclaimed, and rattled off seamless, melodious French. "So why exactly do you need a French translation?"

"Wow." Tish laughed. "Well, in the last year I've been shipping a lot of truffles to Canada. Especially Quebec," she corrected. "I figure why not make it easier for them and offer a page in French rather than force a language on them they don't always use? It would also help to reach another market with another language."

"I understand completely," Lupe said. "I remember learning how to write different languages. It reads so broken and confusing in the beginning." She paused. "I could help you, if you like."

"Really? That would be great," Tish said. "What do you charge for translation services?"

Lupe folded her arms and tilted her head, as though sizing up the price. "Let's see. For a few web pages, that should come to...a home cooked meal, and some good conversation."

Tish laughed. The overture seemed genuine, and inviting. Constant baking and marketing left her little time for socializing, and this might be a nice break in an otherwise busy routine. She pulled a second business card out of her pocket, this one with her home address. "How's Saturday around six?" she posed. "My weekends are generally free."

Lupe held the card between her fingers , flexing the card stock. "Hard to believe, but that sounds good. I can get directions from the Internet. See you then."

Goodbyes exchanged, Tish headed back to her car, feeling a bit better about herself. Things seemed to be falling into the right places this week—new work contracts, strong online sales, and now a new friend. Definitely more than she had last week, yet still missing what she truly craved.

With life on the upswing, she pondered, could love be far behind?

* * * *

"What the—?"

Vinnie plucked the tiny white speakers from his ears, ignoring the tinny music hissing from his MP3 player. He could swear the chassis of the stretch limo above him had inched closer to his face. He wasn't claustrophobic, as he ultimately ended up doing all the dirty maintenance jobs in the garage while the drivers spent their downtime fooling around. Like now, apparently. Yet, he didn't like to be in a situation where he could be killed.

Somebody had slipped into the limo without his knowing. Two bodies, he guessed from the groaning of the undercarriage and the moaning from within the cab.

Shit. Vinnie dug in his heels and pushed with his feet until his rolling platform shot him clean out from under the elongated sedan. Thick droplets of oil stained his white t-shirt, but he paid them no mind. If one of the people he suspected was in the limo rockin', Vinnie imagined she'd want him shirtless and knockin', to either watch in awe or join in on the fun.

I don't think so. On either count. Standing, Vinnie lurched forward and ripped open the passenger side door. The site of Lola—naked, lying on the bench seat with her head toward him, knees spread-eagled—came as no surprise. Cupping her breasts with both hands, she squeezed and pinched the mounds while her neck arched upward. Vinnie watched her oblivious ecstasy flit across her features and flutter her closed eyelids. She mewed and keened while a young driver for Dom named Pete scrunched in the far corner, his face buried in her pussy.

Pete licked her furiously, almost haphazardly by Vinnie's judgment. The poor boy's tongue seemed to twirl like a pinwheel, hitting everything but the sweet spot. Still, Vinnie had no desire to shove the kid aside and demonstrate how it should be done.

Lola opened her eyes, shooting him a smoldering look. She wanted company.

"Let me put that luscious cock of yours in my mouth," she purred.

Vinnie chuckled. She'd never seen it, never would.

Pete must have thought he had been addressed. His mouth detached from her pussy with an audible smack, and Pete began kissing his way up her writhing body. When something dark and round tumbled to the cab floor, Vinnie took notice.

"Watch it!" Wasn't it enough these two were soiling the seats with their cream, they had to add candy to the mix? "We're using this car tonight. Don't mess it up any more."

That's when he noticed the floral pattern on the half eaten truffle, how similar it looked to the candy that had driven him wild yesterday.

He scooped up the chocolate. The half moon rolled in his palm as he brought it to Lola's face. "Where did you get this?" he demanded. He still had a candy left. The girl had better not have been snooping around in his stuff.

"Vinnie," Lola whined.

"Where?" Vinnie took on a forceful tone that visibly rattled Lola.

"Some fat chick was here trying to sell them to us. Like she was a fucking Girl Scout, I don't know."

He might have admonished Lola for her dismissive attitude toward Tish, but Vinnie was at the door to the main office, ignoring the wheedling call of his name.

"Get dressed and get out!" he barked at them over his shoulder.

In the office, he saw only his cousin's wife, enjoying a similar treat. A glance out the window revealed no cars in the parking lot he didn't recognize. He'd missed her.

"Shit!"

He turned to see Lupe's shocked reaction, and felt a hint of heated embarrassment rise to his cheeks. "Eh, *lo siento*," he apologized haltingly. He needed to explain his behavior. "Lola said a woman stopped by to deliver some truffles. Did she make them?"

"Yes. She runs her own business."

Damn. "I was kind of hoping to talk to her."

Lupe smiled. "You wanted to order some?"

Vinnie just shrugged, knowing Lupe was smart enough to catch the deeper meaning of it.

"I see." Lupe remained behind her desk, studying him with amusement. "You like her, then?"

Vinnie grinned. "Well, I like her bonbons," he said as Lupe giggled. "I just wanted her to know that, is all."

Lupe fingered a business card and looked up with a smile. "Okay. If she comes back, I'll let her know."

"*Gracias.*" Vinnie bowed slightly and, as though not sure where to go, barged back into the garage, hoping Lola and Pete had dressed.

"*De nada.*"

Chapter Four

"You didn't have to bring anything for supper," Tish told Lupe on seeing the box in the Brazilian beauty's hands. "I have everything we need in the kitchen."

Tish escorted her to the compact living room, where her active computer setup awaited them. Lupe set the elongated cardboard box on the sofa. "Actually," she was saying, "this is for me. I remembered what you said yesterday about your looks. You didn't sound so sure of yourself."

"Believe me, I am definitely sure of how I look. I just don't like it that much." Tish wanted to wither and blow away like ash off a cigarette. She'd forgotten all about that exchange at the limousine office, and decided to try for a light, devil may care response. "Anyway, sometimes I just ramble about things. It doesn't always represent how I feel all the time."

"Apparently this does," Lupe pointed out. "And there's no reason to bring yourself down about weight and looks. As I told you before, you are very beautiful."

"Uh, thanks."

Lupe lifted the box lid. "I keep hearing on TV ads and the radio about how you can buy the Brazilian secret to beauty in a cream or bottle. It makes me laugh, to think you can get it so easily, when I've had to work at it my whole life. Let me show you something." She pulled out a pair of worn tennis shoes.

"Those are sneakers," Tish said.

"Yes, and they are the Brazilian secret to beauty. You want to know why you always see pictures of gorgeous Brazilian women strolling along the beach? This is why. We don't have cars, we have to walk everywhere we go."

The look of mock exhaust on Lupe's face was too funny for Tish not to laugh.

"Seriously, we love to eat, and we do. I do," Lupe continued. "I wouldn't have asked for dinner in return for helping with your website otherwise." She leaned in closer. "I just don't like to cook."

"Trust me, you've come to the right place," Tish said. "I love to cook, and I hate that I love eating so much."

Lupe patted her shoulder. "You are not fat, Tish. Even by Brazilian standards. You'd be surprised how much attention you'd gain walking through Rio, looking pretty." Lupe batted her eyes.

"Dareville isn't Rio. Not by a long shot."

Lupe didn't offer a rebuttal, but shrugged and said, "I walk the trails at Dareville Memorial Park every morning at seven. I'd love to have a walking buddy to break the monotony. My sister Lola," Lupe rolled her eyes, "prefers to sleep in. It might explain why she's put on a few pounds since she arrived from Brazil."

"Really?" Tish had to wonder how much thinner the young girl was before. "I'd love that, walking I mean. I'm an early bird myself." It would be nice, too, to get out of the house and socialize.

"It'll make a difference, too, even if you don't change your eating habits." Lupe winked. "Now, let's get some translation done. I'm hungry!"

* * * *

Spearing the last bite of cheesy, rippled lasagna noodles, Lupe folded the pasta slowly into her mouth and chewed. A dreamy expression clouded her dark eyes. "As they say in France," she declared, "*magnifique*."

"*Merci*," Tish laughed, clearing their plates. It had amazed her how much of the eggplant lasagna the petite Latina woman had put away in such a short time. Where would it all go later? Tish doubted any of it would end up taking residence on Lupe's hips, as food did with hers, but likely would go for that morning walk and be left behind.

"I have coffee and a sugar-free lemon tart for dessert, if you have room," Tish called from the kitchen. "Nothing fancy, but I had no complaints the last time I served it." *She* hadn't complained at least, Tish remembered, thinking back to the pan she emptied after yet another disappointing blind date.

"Sounds wonderful, please," Lupe's voice chimed in from the dining room. "If you don't mind, while you're doing that I need to check my messages. Robbie probably called and I left my cell in the car."

"No problem." Tish listened for the front door as she prepared two miniature lemon tarts on a puddle bed of blueberry coulis and mint garnish. As she set them on the table Lupe returned, looking a bit ashen.

"I have a flat tire," she announced. "I hope you don't mind that I called the garage to send help over here."

"Okay. Do you need any help with an auto club number or anything?"

Lupe shook her head. "It'll be fine. I meant to say I called my work, the limo office garage. Vinnie is the best mechanic I know. He'll have me out of here in no time."

Tish's heart thudded in her chest. *Vinnie?* Why did that name sound familiar? A few seconds of deep thought over her coffee revived the memory of that delicious Mediterranean hunk she'd met at Jake's.

That Vinnie. *And he's coming here?* Tish's eyes widened at the thought of the gorgeous man with the bronzed arms and piercing brown eyes entering her private space, and felt close to coming herself.

He's welcome to explore other spaces, came the lustful thought. Perhaps a warm, wet cove for an hour or five. Tish decided not to hold her breath on that one.

She barely touched her tart, but merely scraped the tines of her fork across the deep yellow surface and watched Lupe scoop bite after mounding bite of the gelled citrus pastry into her mouth. "I love this," she cooed around a mouthful. "Are you going to sell this at Jake's, too?"

"Uh, not that I know of." Tish locked her gaze on the door behind them. "I suppose I could." How could this woman so casually pork down sweets? A man was coming to the house!

Oh. Tish knew how. Lupe could afford to do it. The woman was married to somebody who worshipped her cocoa butter skin and perfect ass, whereas Tish realized her ass was too big to fit inside one religion.

When the doorbell sounded, Tish started praying for it to decrease at least one dress size.

* * * *

"You didn't have to come." Vinnie glanced tersely at his cousin, keeping his finger depressed on the call button.

Robbie stood slightly behind him to one corner of the concrete pad in front of the door. Arms folded and legs shifting his weight from side to side, Robbie Petrocelli had the look of the quintessential jealous husband. "She didn't *have* to call *you* for help. Lupe is my wife. Yes, I have to be here!" he shot back. The arms fell down to his sides, ending in tight fists. Vinnie made sure to keep an eye on them in case he had to duck.

"Why did she call you instead of me?" Robbie rambled on as they waited for entrance. "I'm her goddamned husband. I should be the one helping her."

"She called a mechanic to fix her car, Rob. You drive cars, you don't repair them as well as I do, and you know that." Weary, Vinnie turned back to the door. If Robbie did hit him, that would mean instant points lost with Lupe. Both men knew it. "Trust me, this is not a slight against you."

"I can change a flat tire," Robbie grumbled. "And why did you throw on a fresh shirt and cologne after she called?"

Damn. Vinnie had hoped nobody noticed that. The second Lupe informed him that she was at Tish Richmond's house, Vinnie's hormones raged into overdrive. No way was he going to show up at his dream girl's house looking and smelling like a slob. He'd been elbow deep in an oil change, and showered as quickly as he could in the locker room Dom had built for the other employees. That Robbie happened to overhear him letting Dom know he had to leave was pure bad luck. He didn't need his cousin thinking he wanted to put the moves on Lupe.

He opened his mouth to speak but the click of a lock jarred him into silence. A rush of cool air from the foyer caressed him as the door opened, revealing Tish Richmond, looking sexy as hell in a pair of knee-length jeans and a deep blue, V-neck blouse. Vinnie relished the taste of air conditioning that provided some relief against the unusually warm evening, yet the sight of Tish caused a tightening in his black jeans that brought him a new level of discomfort.

Not that he minded. Perhaps that would be relieved as well.

"Oh." Tish sounded and appeared surprised. "I'm sorry, I wasn't expecting two—"

"Robbie?" came a chiding voice from deep within the house. Lupe brushed past Tish to the threshold. "What are you doing here? You didn't get my message that I'd be late?"

"I didn't and I'm sorry." Robbie spread his arms wide to invite a reluctant Lupe into an embrace.

When she didn't budge, Robbie gently led her outside to the stone path leading to the driveway. "I was at the office when Vinnie got your call, so I drove him over. I'm going to take you home, and Vinnie'll bring in the car. You can pick it up at work tomorrow."

"What? It's just a flat," Lupe protested. "It won't take twenty minutes to fix. And it's not like I'm stranded in the desert." She gestured back to Tish. "We were having a cup of coffee—"

"Well, it's getting late, and I was worried. Besides, it's better for Vinnie to take the car in case something happens to the tire again on the drive home."

"That won't happen," Vinnie said curtly, embarrassed by the scene his cousin made in front of a now bewildered Tish. "I'm just going to put on the limp tire and take it back to the garage. No big deal, Lupe can drive the car."

Robbie wasn't listening. He stepped forward to offer Tish a grateful bowing gesture. "Thanks for keeping my wife company. I hope you two got everything done that you needed to get done."

"Uh, yeah. Sure," Tish said.

Lupe rolled her eyes and blew out a frustrated sigh. "Fine." She dipped into her purse and tossed Vinnie her keys. "Tish, how about I meet you at the park at seven tomorrow? If the warden will let me out." That last crack was lower, but Vinnie clearly heard it. If Tish did, she kept a poker face.

"Of course." Tish brightened and waved as Lupe slumped into the passenger side of Robbie's car. Vinnie didn't wait for the Prius to disappear completely before turning back to Tish with a lean smile.

The poor thing looked ready to jump out of her skin. What must she be thinking of his crazy family? "Robbie's a nice guy, really. Just a bit protective of Lupe," he said in his cousin's defense.

Tish nodded. "She told me the whole story…of how they met. I understand."

"Cool." Vinnie rocked on his heels, fondling the keys in his right palm. He had to root himself to the spot, at least until Tish made a move back inside the house. One more second and he'd dive sideways to tackle her to the ground and smother her mouth against his in a wanting kiss.

His libido in check, he edged closer to Lupe's car. "I'm going to get started with the, uh, tire," he said. "I got it from here." *Brilliant, Dr. Hawking.* Everything he needed was outside, and now he had no reason to be in her house. She could lock him out.

Tish offered a slight hand gesture and another nod. "Sounds good. I have to clean up and finish a purchase order. Just let me know if you need anything." With that, she disappeared behind the closing front door.

"You bet I will," Vinnie whispered, wondering how he'd be able to kneel comfortably with his raging hard-on.

Chapter Five

"Ugh!"

Baking sheets and metals bowls clattered a disjointed tune as Tish slammed her baking supplies around the kitchen. Could she have been any more like a giggling virgin schoolgirl in front of Vinnie? What must he think of her mooning expression and less-than-seductive nature?

She set a Calphalon pot to boil and retrieved an indented block of bittersweet chocolate from her pantry. Breaking tiny triangles into a glass of bowl, she dared a peek out of the window over the sink. Vinnie already had the back of the car jacked and the lug nuts removed from the faulty tire with that X-shaped wrench—hell if Tish knew what the thing was actually called. Auto repair was not her forte.

But oh, outside of baking, she would definitely choose man-watching as her favorite activity, and she did enjoy spying on this sexy one-man pit crew. Even with the distance, she could detect Vinnie's back muscles rippling underneath the white of his t-shirt, and his tanned biceps flexed and relaxed with little effort as he worked the tire off its axle.

Crud. At this rate he'd be finished, leaving her with little time to work up the nerve to fake a voluptuous persona and invite him in for a cool glass of lemonade to quench his thirst.

"If I had lemonade," she then muttered, realizing her refrigerator contained only diet colas for consumption. Vinnie didn't seem the type for that.

She stripped away a large patch of cling wrap from its roll and tightened it around the glass bowl before setting the whole thing on the bubbling pot. Next she poured a measured amount of whipping cream in a smaller pot to boil on the adjacent flat burner. Once it reached a bubbling point, she would whisk in white chocolate to create what would become the truffle center. The melted dark chocolate, shiny and sweet in its consistency, would serve as a delicious outer shell.

A knock at the door interrupted her concentration and sent Tish's heart pounding. She checked the window—the car remained, limp tire in place, with its caretaker out of sight. That could only mean...

Shit! Quickly washing her hands, she fisted a damp towel and rushed to the door. No time to worry about hair or makeup or clothes. Like Vinnie cared, anyway. This was likely a courtesy ring to let her know he'd be leaving her now. Never to return.

"Hello—" She paused at the doorjamb, expecting to see Vinnie jangling Lupe's keys before her in a casual farewell. Instead her senses knocked backward and she grasped the door for support at the sight of the gorgeous mechanic—shirtless and smiling, his dark eyes glistening with hunger. Thick nipples stood to attention against a smooth chest planed with hard muscle, ridged and curved in all the right places.

"Hey," he said. "What smells so good in there?"

* * * *

He had a pack of industrial strength hand wipes in his back pocket, kept for just such events. They could have sufficed to clean him up, and get the car back to the limo garage without messing up Lupe's car too much. He didn't need to ask Tish for permission to wash before leaving, but damned if he'd let another day pass without expressing his interest in her in some way. Begging the use of her bathroom seemed a legitimate icebreaker—he'd scrub his hands raw with whatever designer soap she probably used until he worked up the courage to ask her out.

But the sweet aroma of chocolate wafting out from within her home struck his senses and brought back memories of her delicious handiwork. He couldn't help but ask.

"Huh?" Tish seemed glazed, distracted. Maybe this was a good sign—removing his shirt, while not necessary for the job, had been an impromptu move for attention. "Y-yes," she said quickly. "I'm making a batch of truffles for Dareville Primary. Fundraiser. Uh, did you want something?" No mistaking the hope in that tone. Vinnie smiled.

"I kinda wanted to wash up," he began, relieved when no further explanation seemed required. Tish ushered him into the foyer and pointed out the half-bath to the side.

"Everything you need is in there," she called, backing into the kitchen on what Vinnie noticed were shaking legs.

Nice. She felt something, too. Perhaps this would go easier than expected if she met him halfway.

Rinsed and dried, he thought to remove the white t-shirt from his other back pocket and redress, then decided against it. That might signal his readiness to leave, and he wouldn't do that without securing at least a date for coffee. Besides, her reaction on seeing him half-naked was too obvious to miss. Best to use all his strengths in catching the tempting Tish.

"You there?" he asked cautiously into the deserted foyer, then followed the rich scent of chocolate into the kitchen, where Tish held vigil over a fancy stove. She looked up at him without a break in her stirring and smiled.

"All set?" she asked. She seemed more relaxed than earlier. Clearly in her milieu she had control.

Vinnie leaned against the doorway, folding his arms. "Yep. Car's fixed, but I'm in no hurry to get back. How are the truffles coming along?"

"Filling's almost done." Tish turned back to the stove and removed a small pot to a metal trivet on the counter. "I'm thinking now I might split this batch and make some of them my signature key lime flavor."

"Nice. How do you do that?"

Tish winked. "Nice try. A good cook doesn't reveal her secret recipes."

"Aw," Vinnie teased. "Can't at least spill one or two of those eleven herbs and spices?"

"Not a granule. Sorry."

"Fair enough." He eyed the wooden butcher's block in the middle of the kitchen, wondering at how much weight it could hold.

And inspiration struck. "Could I have a taste?"

* * * *

You certainly may.

Like *that* would work. "A taste?" she asked instead.

"Of the chocolate," Vinnie said, edging deeper into the kitchen until his abdomen brushed the rim of the butcher's block. Tish stood opposite him, relieved he couldn't see her knees pinned together to keep the lust from rushing between her thighs.

"My mom used to bake cakes and pies all the time," he continued, "and I always got to lick the spoons and bowl." He shrugged, offering a goofy smile. "I dunno, it always made me feel good, like getting a preview of something good."

"Oh, I understand," Tish said. "That's sort of how I became a baker. Only now I try to scrape as much as I can off the utensils."

"Yeah. Every little bit means one more truffle to sell, I'm sure."

"Yep." Tish turned to the bowl of chocolate ganache, stirred the thickening contents, then extracted the wooden spoon. She tapped the base of the curved spoon to release a wide ribbon of chocolate back into the bowl, yet left enough for a free sample. "I'll warn you, though," she said, "eating straight dark chocolate isn't like cake batter. This here is seventy percent cacao, so it's going to have somewhat of a bitter tang, but if you leave it on your tongue long enough you might detect a citrus finish. That's by nature of the particular brand I'm using, which is a single origin from Hawaii. One of the few actually produced there."

"Single origin?"

Tish nodded. "That means the cacao beans used to make this chocolate came from the same place. If you see a chocolate bar that says 'Single Origin Ghana' on the label, for example, you know all the beans came from there," she said. "Sometimes the area is cut even closer. This chocolate was produced at one small farm, that's why I use it. Very high quality."

Vinnie took the proffered spoon, fisting the long, wooden handle at the end. "You sound like you're selling wine instead of chocolate."

"Well, they do go together." Tish laughed. "And gourmet chocolate is serious business. From the way it's grown to how it's prepared. There's more to my job than dipping strawberries in fondue. It's fun, but it takes a lot of research to find the right chocolate for my truffles." She knew she babbled—but she did find comfort in discussing a favorite topic, and Vinnie seemed interested enough not to beg an excuse to leave.

"You have it down to a science, don't you?" he teased. "I'll bet I'd have paid more attention in chemistry if you taught it."

"Me, too. I about flunked it myself."

"What about Home Ec?"

"Never took it, if you can believe that."

Vinnie raised an eyebrow, keeping his gaze trained on her as he brought the dipped end of the spoon to his lips. He held it out far enough that Tish could see the tip of his tongue stroke upward along the concave curve of the spoon and lap up a small trail of the ganache. He moved so simply, so sensually, and inspired a quick fantasy Tish would take with her to bed tonight when she brought her battery-operated friend out for another visit.

"This is awesome," Vinnie said after smacking a thin string of chocolate from the corner of his lip. "I'll buy all the truffles now. How much you planning to raise for the school?"

The comment bemused Tish. "They want to update their library equipment. Digital cameras, new laptops."

"I have one of each. I'll trade," Vinnie joked and waved the spoon. "This is great, really."

Tish waved a finger. "I should try it myself first. It has to past the final taste test before it goes on the truffles."

"Okay, here you go."

Instead of handing back the spoon, however, Vinnie slashed one pec with a streak of chocolate.

Chapter Six

Come on, he urged her silently. *Have a taste.*

He didn't know what had gotten into him, for he normally didn't act so forward with women. One look at Tish, glowing with the passion of her life's work, and those gorgeous breasts swelling under her blouse, and something snapped. Snapped, inflated, surged, whatever. He ached so damn badly for her right now, a mere kiss and request for a date would not appease him.

She looked as though she had gone dry. Her mouth opened and no sound released. The space between them turned suddenly arid and still. If not for the blood pounding in his head, he could swear her heart beat just as loudly.

Yet, it worked. Tish dared a step closer and he helped close the gap by leaning forward. The first touch of her finger against the clumped end of chocolate on his skin sizzled and set off every nerve ending in his body. Imagine what a kiss could do!

She slid her finger across the trail, smearing the chocolate deeper along his chest. "Looks like you spilled...some," she faltered, holding up the covered digit. Vinnie cuffed her wrist and guided the finger to his mouth, taking in the taste of ganache and sweet lavender. His gaze trained on hers, he rolled his tongue around her finger for a few seconds, then released it and her wrist to lean back for her reaction. Stunned, but not affronted, she smiled back at him. He relaxed.

"Would you like some more?" she asked, and eased backward for the stove. To his amazement, she turned off the bubbling pot and grabbed the bowl of dark ganache, all without turning once for guidance.

"You really know your way around a kitchen." Inwardly he cringed at the remark and hoped it hadn't sounded too chauvinistic.

"Among other rooms, yes." She winked. Quite a saucy retort. Vinnie felt glad to have made a move.

Tish dipped that same finger in the bowl and scraped some thickening chocolate from the surface. Reaching up to his face, she smudged his lips with one broad stroke. "Have a taste."

"You, too," he murmured, and pulled her roughly closer for a kiss. Their parted lips met in a crush of chocolate and gasping desire. Vinnie savored the combination of chocolate and Tish's unique flavor as his tongue explored softer depths, guiding her gently into a rhythm that completed with his arms drawing around her waist. Somewhere in the haze he heard the clink of glass against wood. Nothing could distract her from her chocolate— without paying absolute attention, she'd managed to set the bowl safely down on the butcher's block.

He kept his eyes opened and trained on her. Her lids closed and fluttered, as though signaling her becoming lost in their kiss. She seemed to relax and melt into him, and her increasing pleasure showed in the softening lines on her forehead and cheeks. He brushed his thigh against hers, eager to explore more exciting parts of her body.

"Now that I like," he said after breaking free. He reached behind to dip two fingers into the bowl, and beckoned with the sweetness. "Let's try something more exotic," he added, and reached for the top button of her blouse.

To his dismay, she slapped both hands over her throat. "What are you doing?" Her face registered her sudden worry.

"Relax. I just want to taste more of you." He eased one hand away, but not without some effort. Tish cast her gaze away from them, as though looking for one of her kitchen tiles to ripple into an escape hatch. What was wrong? What had happened in the seconds between her enthusiastic kiss and now?

"No," she whispered.

"What?" he prodded, pointing the chocolate-covered fingers at her, aiming for the hollow of her throat. "You don't like it? You want me to stop?"

"No," she repeated, this time sounding weaker. "I don't want you to stop, but…" She swallowed and lifted her face to him, showing glassy tears in her eyes. "You will stop."

"What?" *The hell?*

She hugged herself and stepped back, effectively blocking a direct path to the trail of buttons that hid her bust, and at once Vinnie understood. Being constantly around women like Lupe and Lola, who worked and walked with an air of confidence, he'd come to think that the norm. Tish didn't have a

California toothpick body—not that it bothered him—but he realized *she* might have a problem showing it off.

"Hey. C'mere." He scraped the excess chocolate on the rim of the bowl and moved to lick the rest away, then thought against it. So they'd get dirty. He'd enjoy cleaning up with her.

Tish stiffened in his touch, so he moved slowly and gently to assure her. "Why don't you let me decide if I want to stop?" he suggested. "I can tell you for sure I won't. Feel this."

He brought her free hand down to his crotch and curled it over his rock-hard bulge. "You do this to me just as you are now. Imagine what would happen if you let me sample more of you?"

Tish's eyes widened as she fanned her fingers apart to better cup him. The warmth of that simple gesture caused his cock to throb with greater want. Damn, if he didn't relieve this ache soon his jeans zipper would bust from the pressure. "God, Tish," he groaned.

"I-I'm doing this to you?" She still didn't believe it.

"You can't tell me you don't feel the same way," he said, his voice a hoarse whisper. The hand that had covered hers snaked forward to slip her jeans button from its loop. Metal zipper teeth pried painfully apart, but the sight of pink see-through silk covering a thatch of blonde pubic hair was reward enough.

She groaned in protest.

"What?" he teased.

Tish sighed. "I'm fat."

"You're beautiful."

"I'm wearing granny panties."

"Not for much longer." He loved the shock lighting her eyes at that.

"And I didn't shave this morning—"

"I don't care. Lean back."

He steered her to the block so that the small of her back pressed against the edge. Further protests died on her lips as Vinnie took more control of the situation. He hooked his thumbs under the waist of her jeans at either side and eased them over her hips, hissing with approval with every inch of exposed skin. Granny panties, fleshy thighs, even her pretty polished toenails promised a banquet. When he coaxed the pink silk from her body he saw at least one part was neatly trimmed, barely covering a pussy quivering for his attention.

He scooped up a dollop of ganache and knelt before her, taking in the scent of her desire. She wanted him—her body betrayed her reluctance. He slathered the ganache between her legs but left her pussy untouched.

That single origin he wanted to taste raw first.

* * * *

Oh. My. Fuck. Ing. God!

No way in hell could she have predicted this. She'd prepared only for a nice evening of dinner and conversation with a new friend, and an endless night of truffle making. The dark Italian hunk tickling the juncture between her thighs with his tongue had seemed at best a torrid fantasy to accompany her nightly vibrator session.

158

She peered downward. Yep, he was still there, licking with broad strokes over her skin. Every touch was a stab at her balance — she would drip faster than a bar of Hershey's left in the sun if he didn't stop.

And if he did, she'd protest even more.

Leaning back, elbows bracing on the counter, she closed her eyes and let her body dictate every sensation to her. Heat sizzled and pooled in her belly, sliding down to her pussy where she sensed an explosion any second. Allowing Vinnie to ease her legs apart happened with little effort — he powered her now, and could mold her flesh as simply as she shaped her beloved candies.

With better results, she didn't doubt.

"You taste so damn good, Tish," he murmured over her skin, his lips not breaking contact. Pressing a thumb at the top of her cleft, he pushed the skin upward to expose more of her pussy lips. A light ganache fingerprint tangled in her pubic hair, but she knew his gaze zeroed in on her bare clit.

If only his tongue…oh, there it was!

He lapped at her, so achingly slow, hitting all the right spots. When his other hand rose to explore the depths of her core she noted the ease with which he slipped inside her. She hadn't been this wet in a long time. As he sped the pace of his fingers, she detected her own scent mingling with the chocolate, which assaulted her from the side. Conflicting aromas of sweetness and salt dizzied her senses and distracted her from Vinnie's loving ministrations. She had to get him to bed, away from the busy sensations of the kitchen.

Vinnie shook his head when she quietly suggested it, and kept tapping at her clit. "I like it here," he said when he briefly came up for air.

"I can't keep standing like this," she whined. "It's too much. I'm gonna fall on your face."

Up again. "So do it. I'll catch you."

"I'll crush you."

"I don't care." To assist her, he released his oral hold and rolled onto his seat. Already a wobbling mess, Tish cast a final glance at the chocolate bowl.

Hell, she thought and fisted the dark, bittersweet goop. "Take off your pants," she said, surprised by her rising bravado.

Vinnie obliged with a smile, and soon a large, thick cock saluted from a dark nest of curls. God, but she could create a mold and make a fortune selling chocolate Vinnies to lonely women around the world.

Right. He wanted *her.* She'd share her sacred key lime truffle recipe first.

She pitched forward to straddle Vinnie's hips, then scrambled to reverse herself, all the while tucking in her abdomen so she didn't completely droop like a freakish pendulum. Thank the Lord her breasts were still concealed by her blouse and bra. Doggy style wasn't her most attractive position, but at least with a sixty-nine Vinnie's line of vision would be blocked.

His cock looked too damn good to ignore. She let Vinnie guide her hips and ass to where he could continue eating her pussy, then fisted his shaft with the chocolate, making sure to cover every raised vein and ridge with a thin sheen.

Oh, yeah. Whether the chocolate enhanced Vinnie's natural musk or vice versa, Tish didn't care. The bulbous head of his cock softened between her lips while his rod took on a solid consistency in her grip. Her dry hand cradled his balls, massaging them in circular motion in time to the rise and fall of her head as she reached for every smudge of chocolate. There wouldn't be a stain left, she vowed silently.

"Shit! That's good."

That's what she thought she heard anyway. She wanted to ease up and ask for clarification, but Vinnie strengthened his loving assault on her pussy. The jolt to her core caused her balance to fail, and soon lifting her head to continue sucking him seemed a great effort when the orgasm hit. She writhed atop him, pressing her pussy further back so Vinnie couldn't stop. Side to side he swiped at her clit while fingers probed her cunt and ass, pumping hard.

"Yes!" Seconds after Vinnie's tongue left her, the sensation of pleasure remained strong. Yet her body hadn't recovered when he nudged her to rise.

He muttered and cursed, grasping the floor with glistening fingers until he reached his pants. "Come on, come on, yes!" He successfully fished a wrinkled condom from his now discarded wallet and motioned her to stand. "From behind," he ordered, and ripped a corner of the wrapper. "I wanna see my dick fucking that gorgeous ass."

"Huh?" Up came the uncertainty again, bubbling in her stomach and sliding up her throat in a bitter tang—like a mistaken bite of unsweetened chocolate. He wanted her to bend over the butcher's block? Surely he'd see her so-called gorgeous ass would look more like…big.

She tried to protest but Vinnie had sheathed himself and aimed his cock like a gun. "Turn around," he growled. "I need to be in you, and you need it, too. I can see it."

She didn't doubt Vinnie could read her desire, probably flushed pink across her features. If she turned around, though, he'd see the dimpled cellulite of her backside and the unflattering wide curve of her ass cheeks. There wasn't enough ganache in the bowl to cover her flaws.

Tish didn't argue, though, when he guided her into the right position. She looked over her shoulder and saw huge hands palm her rump, concealing the jiggle. The heat of his skin pulsed over her, warming her in the sudden cool of the kitchen. She twisted back and kept her gaze to her hands, gasping at the first contact of cock to cunt.

Vinnie exhaled audibly, his presence looming large behind her with every push deep into her pussy. Tish had to adjust her stance to better accommodate his girth, and once he fully seated himself she closed her eyes to imprint the sensation in her heart. Shit, it felt good to be filled like this again, and by somebody who called her beautiful. That this happened now still amazed her, however. He didn't blink at her hardly-sexy panties, or the stubble on her shins, or her cottage cheese skin. He was a hunk, a man easily compatible with a woman of equal beauty, like Lupe's flighty sister. Why her instead? Surely he didn't think she was easy and willing to fuck anybody because she thought herself too fat that her options were limited.

Her work kept her from dating, most of the time. Boredom with shallow and uninteresting men prevented a lasting relationship. What if Vinnie turned out like all the others? What then?

The questions nagged her, so much that she hadn't realized Vinnie undid her bra hooks until she sensed his hands cupping her breasts.

Slowly he pumped in and out of her. "I love your breasts," he said on a sigh, and fingered her hardening nipples. "I bet these would taste good on their own."

"Oh, wow." Did she say that out loud? Who cared? Sensation overload loomed imminent. So what if Vinnie turned out to be dull or vain? She'd enjoy the ride, and being ridden.

Head hanging between her braced arms, she thrust her hips backward as Vinnie slammed into her. She was slick, and knew if Vinnie kept the pace he might thrust all the way through her and topple the block. She'd die a happy woman, anyway, not at all disappointed that she'd let Dareville Academy down by not fulfilling their order. So long as they buried her with a box of truffles to go.

"Tish, babe, I'm gonna come." His warning came too late. Seconds later he grunted and pushed his orgasm through her. One hand left her right breast to swirl around her clit as he spilled into her, causing Tish to nearly lose her grip on the counter. She keened and cried her own satisfaction with Vinnie, and moved her hips with his during the slow denouement of their passion, his cock throbbing inside her.

It must have been a full minute as Vinnie rested his forehead on her shoulder, panting heavily. Tish remained still, waiting for her body to slow to the rest of the world before attempting to move. If Vinnie would let her, from his encompassing grasp.

"You know," he said, "only one thing better than eating chocolate is burning it off." He kissed her shoulder.

"Don't I know it."

"Got any more?"

"Oh, yeah."

Chapter Seven

Lupe looked none the worse for wear when Vinnie saw her at her desk. Hopefully Robbie had calmed down last night and cut her some slack.

Humming a happy tune in time to the song on a nearby radio, she clacked quickly away at her computer, looking up only as he set an elegant blue box, dressed in a silk ribbon, on her desk.

He smiled down into her dark, expressive eyes. "Miss Richmond sends her apologies for missing your walking date this morning," he said. "She, ah, had a late night."

Lupe offered him a demure smile. "Is that right?" She glanced at the box, emblazoned with Tish's company's logo. "I've always believed the best apologies were chocolate-covered. Tell her I accept, and that I'll see her bright and early tomorrow for double distance to make up for what she missed."

"You're that confident I'll see her again, huh?" he teased.

"Yes, because you are, too." Turning in her seat, she reached for a stack of note papers. "Here are your messages."

"Thank you. And I have something for you." He reached into his back pocket and produced a thin, shiny object. Lupe opened her mouth to speak but instead gasped on seeing the letter opener bearing the Big Apple logo.

"A bit of advice." Vinnie couldn't help the mirth in his voice. "Next time you have a flat tire, you might want to hang onto the device you used to cause it instead of leaving it under the car. An insurance claims adjuster might get a bit suspicious."

With a sheepish grin, Lupe slid the smooth blade from Vinnie's palm. "I wondered what happened to that."

"You're lucky nobody else got suspicious," Vinnie warned, meaning Tish.

"I won't tell if you won't. Now, if you'll excuse me." Lupe held the opener to a sealed bill. "I have to answer the mail."

Vinnie broke out in laughter and kissed Lupe's forehead. "*Gracias.*"

"*De nada.*"

Get to know Lupe, Lola, Dom and Robbie!
Watch for them in Dare to Dream,
available November, 2008
and Dare Devils, *available mid-2009,*
only at Phaze Books!

Christmas Cake
Victoria Blisse

Also by Victoria Blisse

Proving Santa Exists
Getting Physical
Masquerading Hearts
Naughty Rendezvous
Phaze in Verse

"Flaming Hot" from
Coming Together Under Fire

"Till the End"
from *39 and Holding…Him*

"Reluctant Muse"
from *Phaze Fantasies, Vol. V*

Curvaceous (print collection)
Sweet Surrender
Seasons of Blisse
Making it Real

"I'll have half a dozen of your mince pies as well, please, Emily."

"Sure, Mrs. Tanner. You're starting early this Christmas."

"Oh, well it's not that far off now, is it? I've got the family coming on Saturday and I'm doing a bit of a spread. Karen wouldn't forgive me if I didn't put out some of your mince pies."

I blush, picking out the rest of the order and putting them into a stiff, white paper box.

"Well here we are, Mrs. Tanner." I look down on the mince pies, the small brown loaf, and the half a dozen oven bottoms. "That'll be four pound eleven."

"Thanks, Emily, see you next week." Mrs. Tanner passes me the cautiously counted out coins and I drop them into the till.

"Goodbye, Mrs. Tanner." I call then, rearrange the display of mince pies. Looking out of the glass front door, I can see the twinkling lights and tinsel in the window of the fashion shop opposite. I shake my head, it's only just crept into December, the air has still got the mellow crispness of autumn lingering on it, yet the Christmas display has been out for a month across the road already.

I start selling mince pies on the first of December now, simply because of demand. The fruitcake doesn't come out until at least a week before Christmas Eve and the gingerbread trees and Santas will be baked for the first day of the children's Christmas holidays when I will put up my decorations.

When I was a little girl Christmas didn't start till Christmas Eve and my family were bakers even then, but as the years have passed it's gotten earlier and earlier, with the big shops starting to sell Christmas gifts as early as October these days. I know I sound like a grumpy old woman, but that's because I am a grumpy old woman and Christmas doesn't mean anything to me now.

When Greg was alive Christmas was the most magical time of the year. He loved Christmas. We'd sing Christmas carols as we baked, we'd have this massive meal, inviting all those who would otherwise be alone at Christmas, and it was always a full house. But Greg died ten years ago and I've become one of those alone at Christmas.

We never got to have kids. We had plans, but it just seemed that Mother Nature wasn't keen on helping us along. It wasn't a burning desire for either of us, but now I'm completely alone and I physically ache with want for a child, someone to remember Greg with. I keep the bakery on my own, I bake what people want for Christmas, but I don't even put up a tree in my flat above the shop.

The door bell tinkles and I look up.

"Wow, it smells delicious in here." His rumbling voice suits the tall, imposing body it is attached to.

"Thank you, sir."

"Oh, call me Jim, please."

"Okay, Jim." It is unusual to find yourself on first name terms with a brand new customer, but his open smile and easy manner make me feel as if it's the most natural thing in the world.

"I'm new 'round here," he states, his bright blue eyes scanning the shelves before him as he talks. "I just moved in over the road."

"Well, welcome." I smile and his gaze flicks from the display of cream cakes and fixes on me.

"Well, thank you, oh, what is your name?"

"Emily," I reply.

"Thank you, Emily." He holds out his hand above the high counter top and I reach mine over. He takes it in his strong grip and shakes it, my stomach shakes in time.

"So, have you moved here with family?" I ask, as he continues to visually devour my cake display. "Oh no, it's just me. I've got a new job here, and at my age you got to go where you're needed."

"Oh yes. I just hope I can keep this place going, I am far too old to be searching for jobs now."

His eyes meet mine again and I feel my cheeks pinking on their own accord.

"Oh, no, that can't be true. A vibrant young lady like you is just in her prime of life, surely."

"Why, thank you." I flush more and look down at the cakes in the display before me. "But I am definitely over that hill these days."

"Well, as long as we're both on the same side of the hill, I'm happy."

He grins and I laugh. "Right, I think I've finally decided. I'll have a mince pie, please, and one of those delicious looking vanilla slices."

"Certainly, anything else?" I ask as I take a breath and try to keep my hand steady as I handle the delicate pastries.

"Oh, and a small tin, please."

"Would you like that sliced?"

"Oh no, I prefer to cut my own, you know. I'm old fashioned like that."

"Oh, I'm the same." I pull a small white loaf from the shelf behind me and wrap it in stiff paper.

"That will be one pound seventy eight please, Jim."

He passes me the exact change and takes his goods with a wink.

"I'll see you again soon, Emily. I'll not be able to stay away from such sweet treats."

"Goodbye," I call after him, wondering exactly which treats he was talking about.

* * * *

"Yes, Mrs. Clatterbridge," I speak into the receiver. "I'll make sure it's just how you like and I'll deliver it on Christmas Eve for you, not a problem. Goodbye."

I slam down the receiver and return to the shop window. Decorating is something I have to get done after the early rush and before the lunchtime shift. I've never been one to work out of work hours — my father always said that that was a sure fire path to a heart attack. I've got the Christmas tree up. It's a case of testing the lights now and placing the last few decorations beneath the tree.

I reach behind me for the plug socket just behind the window display — it should only take a short stretch to reach it. I yelp as my hand brushes against another and the lights flicker into life.

"Jim, what on earth are you doing? I didn't hear you coming in."

"I'm sorry. I was just trying to help." He grins. "The tree looks beautiful."

I stand up and tut, but he is right about the tree. It looks beautiful covered in my hand made gingerbread decorations, tinsel and baubles. "You've done a great job."

"Thanks, so what are you after today?"

"Oh, I don't know. I'm always spoilt for choice in here my dear."

His smile is a spell that takes over my mind. I forget all my upsets, my anger and fear and I smile back, my mind absorbed in the happiness being transmitted from his lifted lips.

"Well, I do my best to please my customers."

"Oh, and you always do, Emily, you always do. What time do you get up to bake all these delights?"

"Four AM," I reply, "But then I've never been much of a sleeper."

"It's amazing, such dedication."

"Oh," I wave my hand dismissively, "it's just part and parcel of the job."

"You're a treat, Emily. A sweet treat, and I'll take a rum truffle today I think, and my bread."

"Certainly," I said "A good choice. How's the new job going?"

"Oh, it's going," Jim replies, shrugging his shoulders. "I've not seen any excitement yet, but I suppose I might have more luck come the January sales."

"Oh yes," I laugh, "You must especially look out for Mrs. Tibbs, she's a complete beast when it comes to sales."

"Really? She's not but a drink of water, that one."

"Oh, it's the quiet ones you've got to watch."

"Thanks, I'll add that to my security guard manual." He grins, tipping his black peaked hat to me.

"I'll see you tomorrow, sweetheart."

"Ta ra," I reply, waving as he walks out of the shop, the bell jingling loudly. It's a moment before I realise my hand is still raised and I pull it quickly to my side.

"Emily," I scold myself, "pull it together, you simpering idiot." And I get back to decorating the bakery. When Greg was alive we had so much fun as we put up the decorations. Not a corner was left empty—even in the back, around the ovens and the work tables, we would have bunches of holly and mistletoe mixed in with tinsel and plastic Santas.

Not now. No, the decorations stick to the front of the bakery, not a sprig is to be found in the kitchen or the little flat upstairs. Christmas is a miserable time, I miss Greg, I miss my mum and dad and I miss my friends. I realise just how lonely I am every year at Christmas time, I hate it.

But I keep going, I have to. I'm a baker, it's the only thing I know, and what else could I do? If I went on holiday, I'd still be miserable, if I didn't open the shop I'd be bored. So, every morning I paste on my smiliest smile and I wish the world a Merry Christmas and I mean it. I do hope people enjoy their

Christmases with friends and family and good cheer. I wish I'd appreciated mine more when I had them. I sure miss them now they're gone.

* * * *

The Salvation Army Band is playing, the shop has been full to bursting all day — it's Christmas Eve. Every year it still surprises me how many people leave their shopping right to the very last minute. I've come to the conclusion that they enjoy the stress. Why else would you put yourself through it?

"God rest ye merry gentleman..." I chirp, the sound of the band getting louder.

"Let nothing you dismay." A male voice booms.

"Oh, you have a wonderful voice, Jim"

"Well, thank you Emily, Merry Christmas."

I paste on my smile, "Merry Christmas, Jim. Have you come for your cake?" I have put aside my best cake for Jim. I took hours decorating it, and it looks quite stunning even if I do say so myself.

"Oh no, I've got a few more hours on yet, I just popped in for something sweet on my break."

"Well, I'm afraid there isn't much left. I'll be closing up in a few hours."

"Oh, I am sure that you'll have something to satisfy me, sweet Emily."

I flush and he winks.

"Are you off to your family for Christmas, or are they coming to you?"

"Oh, yes. I'm going there, away. Yes, they'll pick me up later."

I lie. It's a terribly thing to have to admit to, being alone on Christmas Day.

"I'll be back the day after Boxing Day, though."

"Oh, good, I'll miss you. Enjoy your Christmas."

"I will." My smile is still stuck on, my heart is sighing.

"Well, I'll just take a currant slice and get back to work. I'll be by at five for my cake."

"Okay, Jim. If I'm closed just knock."

"Okay, I will. When will you be going, I don't want to miss out on my cake."

"Oh, not 'til much later, don't worry."

"Fair enough, Emily. See you later!"

He takes his paper bag, leaving the money on the counter top.

"O tidings of comfort and joy, comfort and joy. O tidings of comfort and joy."

The music and his voice echo round my shop as he leaves and I feel a small teardrop land on my cheek. I wish I had a little comfort and joy.

The last of my day's customers keep me busy. Christmas cakes and mince pies leave along with fondant fancies, snowy iced stolen slices and festively decorated biscuits. I make more money on this one day of the year than I make in some whole weeks at other times. I should be happy, but I cannot raise a true smile, for tomorrow I will be completely on my own.

I stay open till a little after five, waiting for Jim, but as the shop is all but sold out, I decide to turn the sign and begin the nights tidying. Just as I do, someone barges in the door.

"Hey, be careful, I was just going to close."

"I don't care." A falsely gruff voice barks at me and I find a sharp point at my nose.

"All your money, in this bag, now or else." The voice continues, stabbing the long, sharp knife in my direction.

My hands fly up in defense.

"S...S...Sure." I stutter, walking behind the display cases.

"No funny business."

"No, of course not."

"Just empty the cash into here, quick."

I take the proffered bin liner and ping open the till. My hands are shaking and my mind is whirring, but I can't help but think I recognize the voice hidden deep within the depths of that dark hood.

I start with the change, buying myself some time. I pray earnestly for a miracle and suddenly I hear an impact of flesh on flesh, a clattering and a familiar voice.

"Well then, what do you think you're doing?"

It's Jim, and he's got the robber trapped in his muscular arms.

"Oh, Jim, thank God," I cry and he nods at me.

"Ring 999, Emily. Go on, there's a good girl."

"No!" the hooded figure screams, his real voice now uncovered, "Oh, Emily please, no."

I walk round to the front of my shop.

"Emily, he's dangerous, what are you doing?"

"He's not dangerous." I shake my head, taking the rim of the hood in my hand and throwing it back "Scared maybe, but not dangerous."

A sheepish young face appears, smudged black, the dark hair shiny with grease and the eyes shining with fear.

"Jack Bailey," I hiss, "what on earth do you think you're doing?"

"Oh, Emily, I'm so sorry, but our Charlie really wants this princess doll house thing. But it's so much money, and I can't afford it. Emma and I have tried to save up, but Emma's packing job doesn't bring in much and my benefit is even less. Oh, Emily, we have tried to save but we've nowhere near enough for it. I was gonna bring back the money I didn't spend, oh Emily. I'm so sorry."

"Ring the police." Jim reiterates, his grip not loosening, his tone harsh.

"No, I will not." I snap. "Let him go."

"No, I won't!" Jim splutters, "Emily, he'll run away."

"Not if he knows what's good for him and his family, he won't."

Jim sighs and loosens his grip.

"Right, Jack, come here."

I open the till and take out five crisp, twenty pound notes.

"This is your wages." I look at the scared boy, his eyes shining, his face covered with confusion. "I'm giving you an advance. I expect you here at five AM precisely on the twenty-seventh of December, you hear? You're going to be my apprentice.

"Really, Emily?" His eyes are wide, and his dirty face cracks into a smile.

"Really, Jack, this is your first week's wages. I know it's not much, but it'll increase as you learn and you can help me more."

"Emily, Emily, thank you." Tears stream down his cheeks and he dashes them away with the back of his hand.

"I remember you as a lad, Jack. You were such a good boy and you always looked after your Mam, God rest her soul. Make her proud, lad. Look after your lovely wife and delightful daughter and make something of yourself, you can do it, I know you can."

"I will, Emily, I'll be here. I'll do you proud, I will and Mam and Emma and little Charlie."

"Here," I pass him the money, "and you might as well have these, too." I pack up the last cakes in a box and pass them over. "Merry Christmas, Jack."

"Merry Christmas, Emily. I'm so sorry I..."

"Water under the bridge, son, don't mention it no more. See you in two days, okay?"

"Oh yes, Emily, five sharp."

He smiles and ducks round Jim and leaves the shop, whooping with delight.

"So, did you come for your cake this time?" I smile at Jim and he shakes his head.

"Well, I never," he exclaims. "Do you really think he'll turn up for work?"

"Yes, I think he will, Jim. Jack's a good lad. He lost his mum just in the year his little one was born, it broke his heart. He's a good lad, is Jack, He'll see me proud, I'm sure."

"He pulled a knife on you." Jim shakes his head and I walk round to change the sign to closed, as I'd intended to before.

"Desperate men do desperate things, Jim. He wouldn't have harmed me."

"I can't believe this, I really can't." He shakes his head once more. "I didn't know you had a job going."

"Oh, I don't. I don't make that much, but I can't look after this place alone forever as I have no kids." I shrug, "I might as well train someone to follow in my footsteps."

"I thought…" Jim looks puzzled. "Where are you going for Christmas, then?"

"Nowhere." I sigh, wiping a hand across my face. "I lied to you, Jim. I'm sorry. I'll be here, home on my own, but I don't like telling people that."

"Oh, Emily." Jim puts his hand gently on my shoulder, "You're a wonder."

A tear slides down my cheek and his hand squeezes. "I'll not see you on your own, no. You can come over to mine."

"Oh, I couldn't possibly intrude on your family gathering." The tears are flowing steadily now, and I lift my hand to bat them away, his touch still firmly pressing on my shoulder.

"You won't be," he replies. "I'm going to be on my own, too."

"Oh," I sniff, "well, okay then." I smile and he laughs.

"We'll have a wonderful time. Now, shut up shop and come round."

"Now?"

"Well, yes, now. I'm not having you on your own a moment longer."

"Oh, but I can't…"

"Oh, but you can. I'll sleep on the couch. Pack an overnight bag and come on, there's no need for us both to be lonely, is there?"

"No, you're right." I determinedly walk to the till and begin to count the takings. "We might as well enjoy it. Christmas comes but once a year, right?"

"Exactly." Jim grins. He follows me as I walk upstairs.

"I'll just quickly pack an overnight bag." I chatter away nervously, very aware of his tall, stocky frame behind me.

"There's no rush, Emily. I'm not in work now till Boxing Day and I'm just going to take it easy."

"Oh, and remember to take your Christmas cake," I yell through from my bedroom. "What to take?" I mutter under my breath, trying to clear my thoughts and concentrate on the task in hand. I've not been invited out of my bakery in years apart from Church and the occasional outing with them. Now, I can't even remember the last time I was invited out by a gentleman friend.

I press some underwear, a nightdress, and some clothes into a bag. I remember my toothbrush and head across to the bathroom to get it.

"Oh, Emily." Jim sighs as I walk into the living room. "I didn't realize."

"What, Jim, what is it?" I stop in my tracks, my overnight bag dropping to the floor beside me.

"The shop is so full of Christmas, your mince pies taste of it, your window shines out and shows some real Christmas Spirit, but inside, inside Christmas is dead." He shakes his head and lets out a shuddering breath.

"I used to love Christmas." I walk to the sofa and sit down, my body collapsing as my well-constructed lie falls down around me. "I really did, it was my favorite time of the year. As a kid we had the best Christmases. My parents weren't well off, but we always had a wonderful meal and mum and dad always made sure I got the toy I most desired."

Jim sits beside me, his thigh brushing mine.

"Then when I married Greg, the Christmas Spirit still reigned. We never had children of our own but we loved seeing the children as Christmas approached. We would give out free cookies to the kids on Christmas Eve, and I still remember their excited smiles and the thank yous and the happy sound of them crunching on our sweet treats." I let out a reluctant breath, my eyes fill with tears, and I tangle my fingers together on my lap.

"When Greg died, ten years ago, it was near Christmas. I remember walking home after he passed away, cancer took him from me." I shake my head as tears fall down my cheeks and I feel Jim's hand on my arm, comforting me. I can't look at him, though, I just stare at the wall in front of me. "I walked back to the shop through fairy-lit streets, Christmas trees, snowmen and Santas watching me and then I knew...I knew it was all a front. Christmas meant nothing. It couldn't cure my husband, it couldn't bring me the child I longed for, it's just a drain on people's resources, an excuse to over indulge." I shrug my shoulders, and feel Jim's arm wrap around me.

"I didn't realize you were so alone," he whispers, squeezing me.

"Oh," I sniff, looking up for the first time into his soft baby-blue eyes, "I'm not that alone, really. I see people every day, stop and chat with them. It's not a bad life."

"Well, there's no use crying over spilt milk, eh? Let's get over to mine and see if we can find that Christmas Spirit of yours, eh?"

"Yeah," I smile at him, sniffling, "yeah but I warn you, I've kept it buried for many years, I don't think it's going to be easy to find—I've lost all faith in Christmastime."

"Don't worry," he squeezes me to him again, my heart pounding, "I've got enough for two."

* * * *

"It's like Santa's grotto in here." I laugh as I wander into Jim's small but Christmassy flat.

"I love Christmas." He blushes. "Reminds me of being a kid and well, I'm a big kid at heart."

"It's lovely." I beam and I mean it. I'm not happy that I've lost all my Christmas spirit. It's good to see someone keeping it so alive. There is barely a surface in the small living room that isn't covered in tinsel or fairy lights or Christmas cards or candles.

"I'll put your bag in the bedroom, then I'll serve up some tea for us both." Jim smiles and opens a door off to the right. I take a long deep sniff, and realize the delicious smell that I had been commenting on all the way up the stairs was in fact coming from the tiny kitchen at the end of the room.

"Jim, what are you cooking, it smells delicious."

"Oh," he yells from the bedroom, "it's just a simple stew I've done in the slow cooker, that thing is a God send." He walks back into the living room dressed in jeans and a white t-shirt. A fresh breeze of citrus and musk floats past as he walks into the small kitchen.

"Do you need a hand?" I ask, but he shakes his head.

"Nah, oh, well, you can set the table if you like."

So, whilst he serves out two bowls of warm, comforting beef stew I pull up the leaf of the table and put out mats and cutlery.

"Oh, I'm ready for this," I sigh as he puts the bowl down in front of me. "I've not stopped all day."

"Oh, I know what you mean. I'm glad for the day off tomorrow, that's for sure."

We sit in companionable silence which is broken only by the odd groan of satisfaction as the stew in our bowls slowly disappears along with chunks of fresh, white bread from the bakery.

"Now, Emily, I'm going over to church tonight for Midnight Mass, will you join me?"

I was about to say no, listening to Christmas carols had become so painful, but something stopped me.

"Jim, I want to try, but I don't know if I can do it. The carols are so uplifting and joyful and it's so long since I felt able to listen let alone join in with them."

"I know." Jim puts down the bowls and places his hand on my shoulder, "but I know, well at least I think, that a person like Greg wouldn't like to think of you being so miserable at this time of year especially."

"I know." Tears well up in my eyes and I sniff them back, "I know and I'm going to try to change now for Greg's sake, and for my sake. I want to be able to live again, Jim."

Jim smiles and bends his head. My heart thumps as his face comes down closer to mine and, although his lips simply caress the flesh on my forehead, my whole body zings to life with a sensual buzz that's been missing from my life for so many years.

"Well, there are a few hours till Mass, let's see what's on the telly, eh?"

"A good idea." I grin, mentally shaking myself. *Snap out of it, he's just being friendly. Just because you've not been laid in ten years, doesn't mean you are ready to be laid now, young lady.*

* * * *

I'd always had a zesty appetite for sex. I felt I was lucky to have found an excellent sexual match in Greg, but when he died, so did my libido. It is amazing that after all this time desire seems to have found its way back to me. Jim is a new friend, and someone I've opened up to. Maybe because he has none of those pre-conceived images of me being the strong, coping widow. I never let anyone know how I really felt inside. I've not got anyone else I talk to about how I feel inside, never did. Greg was the only person who really knew me, and I shared all my hopes, dreams and fears with him. I mustn't jeopardize this newfound understanding between me and Jim. So keeping my urges deep inside might be a good thing.

I try to ignore the image of Greg in a Santa outfit, his cock out and my lips just kissing its tip. As I shake that memory away I try equally as hard to banish the flash of him naked, his erect cock tied round with a big, red bow.

"Oh, *Scrooge* is on, you know the musical one." Jim places the remote control on the coffee table and eases himself down onto the sofa.

"Oh, the one with Albert Finney? That's my favorite." He nods and pats the seat next to him on the sofa. I walk over and sit down, a foot or so away from his body. This far away I still have hope of being able to think straight without my hormones getting in the damn way. I try to get into the film I've seen a thousand times.

"Ah, it's really Christmas now." He grins and I'm sure he moves closer as his body heat seems to suddenly envelop me.

"Oh, yes. Christmas Eve is when Christmas starts, no matter what the retail market will try and have us believe." I nod, realizing I sound more and more like my mother with every passing day.

"I quite agree. I feel sorry for the mothers and fathers of kids who are wound up about Christmas a month or more in advance these days. In my day we wrote our letter to Santa a week or so before and the tree and trimmings went up on Christmas Eve."

"Same here," I smile, "and the beauty of the season was so fresh and exciting. It was unheard of for people to be fed up of Christmas before it's even begun." I open my mouth to continue and, listening to how we sound, I laugh instead. "Oh, Jim, we do sound like a pair of old fogies, don't we?" Our laughter whips together, his deep note highlighted by my tinkling giggle. "When did I get old?"

"You're not old," he whispers, his face just in front of mine, his thigh gently pressed against my own. How did he get so close? "I'm not old and you're younger than me."

"Oh, you flatter me, Jim, but I sure do feel old." I sigh, feeling my forty-five years hanging heavily upon me.

Jim's hand reaches out and caresses my cheek. "You don't feel old to me," he smiles.

I can hear his breathing as I wander through the frosty gateway to his soul, his gaze pulling me to him. His large hand barely touching my flesh is setting my cheeks alight and the flames are licking up and down my whole body, eagerly devouring me.

My hand reaches up to cover his, to pull it away or make a point or something quite important, I'm sure, but it just rests there, enjoying the warmth and detail of his warm hand as his lips move in and soon enough (yet seemingly in agonizingly slow motion) press against my own.

It's so soft, so gentle, so sensual and so poignant at first. It is like a whisper, a gentle hint as we rest together, not moving, just joined and hesitantly enjoying the feel of being so intimate with another person. He makes the first move, his hand slipping down to rest on my shoulder as his mouth palpitates against mine. My lips part and I taste him, heavy with gravy and meat and with a spicy masculinity that is all his own. My mouth responds, my hands fall to my sides as all my energy and attention is focused in on my lips, moving them up and down, forward and back and creating the most delicious friction against his plump, slick lips.

"Jim," I gasp as he pulls away slightly, "I can't think…"

"Then don't." he interrupts, his mouth crushing mine whilst his tongue invades and his arms embrace me, I feel his warmth surrounding me and I panic and push away.

"I can't, Jim, I'm not ready."

Jim pulls back immediately, the gap between us returning. "I'm sorry, Emily, I'm not sure what came over me there, I shouldn't have pushed my advantage."

He crosses his arms over his chest and pointedly looks back to the TV, negativity radiating from every inch of his body.

"Sorry," I whisper, taking a deep breath. He shrugs and doesn't even look away from the TV.

"Don't worry about it. You're not ready. I made a mistake."

I don't reply, but I know who made the mistake and it wasn't Jim.

* * * *

The walk up to the church is awkward, the silence stretching between Jim and me almost to breaking point. There is cold sharpness to the air — there will be a thick layer of frost by the morning, but right now there is just the faint shimmer of it skimmed over the exposed surfaces of the street and the houses lining the street.

The number of people flowing towards the church amazes me. There is a buzz of conversation around us, the expectancy is contagious.

"Y'alright, Jim?" A frail old voice comes from the other side of the road.

"Oh, hey Harry. I'm alright, how are you?"

"Fine." The old man crosses the road and the two old friends continue to chat. As we walk up the path to the church I freeze. Jim only takes a step more then notices I've stopped.

"I'll see you in there, Harry."

"Aye, alright." He smiles, tipping his flat cap in my direction.

"I can't go in." I shake my head vigorously. "I really can't go in."

"Well, you don't have to." He smiles, his hand resting on my arm. "I'm going in, though. Come and stand in the porch at least, or you'll freeze."

I nod my head and he puts a guiding hand on the top of my arm and gently pulls me forward. I take a deep breath and move through the stone archway. Jim squeezes my arm, making my tummy tumble over and giggle coyly.

"I'll be just at the back there if you change your mind." He bends and kisses my cheek, gently. "I'm sorry." Then he walks off and I'm left wondering exactly what happened just then.

Greg was a great man, but he'd never apologise because he was never wrong, or so he believed, and well, I think I just got an apology from someone who hasn't actually done anything wrong. Oh, damn-it-all, men are frustrating. I want to talk to him and he's standing casually by the back pew just chatting with a group of fellow church goers, so why can't I just walk in and talk to him?

I guess when Greg died I blamed God. I still needed Greg here with me on earth, so why was he taken away from me? I didn't lose my faith, I just gained a dislike for it. I've not talked to God since then and I think walking into His house after such a long time might prove to be uncomfortable.

But I need to talk to Jim. I've got to let him know he's done nothing wrong. I make a slight movement forward just as the priest's voice echoes through the long stone hallway, welcoming people to this special service and I stay in place. I look over to Jim and he's looking straight at me. He waves and I blush, waving back before falling back into the cold shadows.

Just the smell of musty hymn books and ancient stone makes me shiver. Greg and I had spent many hours in the church, it was part of our life and our routine, but it's been such a long time since I last walked through the door. However, right now I feel something drawing me in. Maybe it's the warmth of the congregation because it is as cold as ice out here but no, I think it's more than that.

I can hear the Christmas readings, the carols and feel the wave of light-hearted giddiness flowing from inside to outside, pulling me in. I've held my grudge far too long and now I begin to wonder why I'd locked all this goodness out of my life.

Because I wanted to be miserable, I wanted to mourn, to be bitter and alone because I love Greg so much. But I can see him now, his smile gentle and warm, his head shaking from side to side but his eyes lit with love and compassion.

He doesn't want me to be miserable. He only ever wanted to see me happy. Why has it taken me ten years to realize that my unhappiness would break his poor heart. He lived to make me smile, so why disappoint him now?

A high voice begins to belt out a hymn, and the words pull me in to the church. I step over the threshold and listen:

Till He appeared and the soul felt its worth,
A thrill of hope the weary world rejoices,
For yonder breaks a new and glorious morn;
Fall on your knees, Oh hear the angel voices!
O night divine, O night when Christ was born!

I'm pulled towards the nativity scene, sitting serenely at the back of the church. I walk towards the wooden stable, Mary and Joseph looking down proudly on a smiling babe, lying in a trough of hay.

"I'm sorry," I whisper, a tear falling down my cheek as I stare at the smiling baby boy.

The King of Kings lay thus in lowly manger.
In all our trials born to be our friend.
He knows our need, He guardeth us from danger
Behold your King! Before Him lowly bend!

I lower my head, my heart full of emotion. Finally, I'm letting go of a grudge I should never have born in the first place, and losing the weight is almost painful at first as I stretch out what has been repressed for so very long.

Truly He taught us to love one another
His law is love and His gospel is peace.

I feel my breast fill with heat, the love held so long in check blossoms once more and it doesn't hurt. I open up the love that belonged so long to my husband, the love that we shared, and it feels good to remember and re-feel the miracle of a heart filled with passion and joy.

I feel a strong arm around my shoulder and look up into the bright blue of Jim's eyes. I swing into his embrace and he holds me tight as I sob into his chest.

"I'm not sad," I gasp as I lift my face, coming up for breath. "I'm just full of emotion, full to overflowing."

Jim nods, and continues to hold me close. "Feeling better now?" he asks.

"So much better," I smile, "oh so very much better."

"Merry Christmas, Emily."

"Merry Christmas, Jim." I laugh because this time I really mean it.

* * * *

"I'm so tired." I yawn as we walk back to Jim's little flat. "This is the first time I've seen midnight in a very, very long time."

"Same here," Jim smirks, "let me just get my stuff from the bedroom and we'll get to bed."

I follow him into the bedroom, where he is stretching up to the top of the wardrobe and pulling down a pillow and duvet.

"I feel really bad about kicking you out of your bed, you know."

"Oh, don't be silly." He smiles. "Where else could you sleep?"

"But it seems so unfair of me to kick you out of your lovely, big warm bed."

"Well, it is a big bed." He grins, placing the duvet on a chair in the corner and stepping towards me.

"Yeah, it is a big bed, and it's made for two." I feel the blush heat my face.

"And I think we're grown up enough to be able to share a bed, right?"

Jim looks almost as nervous as I feel. His lower lip is clasped between his teeth and his cheeks are flushed.

"I think we could, I mean, if you're okay with that," I add.

"Sure." He laughs. "You don't snore do you?"

"Uhm, I don't think so. I can't listen to myself sleep."

He laughs and puts the duvet back on top of the wardrobe.

"I'll just go and get ready for bed." I pick up my overnight bag and head for the bathroom. "I won't be long."

"Okay." He smiles, and I see him grasp the bottom of his t-shirt, lifting it to expose the soft under-curve of his stomach. I turn quickly and walk out of the room before my libido explodes and makes a mess all over the bedroom carpet.

It's amazing how much can change in just a day. I'm in a new friend's bathroom preparing to climb in his bed. I've been held at knifepoint and given my attacker a job. Yes, days like this don't come round very often. I regret my choice of nightwear now, but I really just pulled out the first thing that came to hand.

It's not only that it is a shapeless, floral nightdress with old fashioned lace at the collar and cuffs, but looking at myself in the bathroom mirror I notice that the material is almost transparent, if it weren't for the tactfully placed pink posies, I'd be showing off more than I'd be hiding. Well, there is no time for regret, now.

I run over to the bedroom, take a breath, and open the door. I walk over to the bed and leap in it without even noting where Jim is in the room.

"Well, I've never had a woman so eager to get in my bed before." He laughs even more when I look up and find Jim clad only in his underwear. I try my hardest not to stare at his tanned torso or anything lower than that, either.

"Well, I'm a bit embarrassed by my nightwear," I admit.

He chuckles. "So, when I tell you I can't sleep on any other side of the bed than the one you're on, you're not going to be happy, are you?"

"Oh, right, shall I shuffle over, then?"

"If you don't mind," he replies, grinning.

"Sure, yes, of course." I find it impossible to move over with the blankets clenched to my chin, and so I have no choice but to let them drop to my waist. I hear his sharp intake of breath as I move over, and I keep my eyes lowered to the navy blue bedspread, but I can't help but notice the swelling beneath his boxers as I lower my gaze.

"Thank you." He steps over to the bed. I keep my eyes trained on the bedspread as he lifts the blankets and lies down next to me.

"Have, have you got enough room?" I stutter, smoothing down the cool cotton with my shaking fingers.

"Oh, plenty," he replies. "Shall I turn off the lamp?"

"Uhm, yes, please." I relax as everything goes dark and I wriggle down below the covers. "Well, goodnight then." I face towards the wall, my back to him.

"Goodnight, Emily. Sweet dreams," he replies and the room goes quiet, not silent as I can hear my own breath and the dull tick-tock of the alarm clock. I close my eyes and attempt to sleep, it should be easy. I'm tired and it's well past midnight, but like a child I find sleep just will not come. I close my eyes tighter and will myself to sleep, like I did when worried that Santa would not come if I didn't sleep, but I just can't nod off and now I'm uncomfortable.

The more I try to relax the more it seems to irritate me. I can't lay like this anymore. I'll have to roll over. It'll be okay, Jim will be asleep by now surely and a new position might just be all I need to drop off.

I turn over and end up nose to nose with Jim, but before I can apologise I feel his hand rest on my hip and his head tips and he's pressing his lips to mine. My mind goes blank. The apology is wiped away by the insistence of his kiss and the weight of his fingers as they lie on my hip. My hand presses out and rests in the hair of his chest. My fingers trail through the springy forest and the gurgling groan it elicits thrills through my body like electricity through an open circuit.

I don't know if I moved closer to him or vice versa or if we were pulled together, but my arm moves up and over to his shoulder as his chest presses up against my own. His hair tickles me through the light nightdress and my breath catches at the back of my throat. His lips slip down from mine and trail across my cheek and over my chin, dipping down onto my neck, and every fiber screams, wanting more. It's like I've been lost in the desert and I've trickled the first drop of water onto my parched tongue, wetting it and making it thirsty for more.

"What, what are we doing, Jim?" I groan as he nibbles on the place where my neck and collarbone meet.

"Making love." He groans, pulling his hand up and taking a fistful of nightdress with it.

I'm going to question more but his hand slips onto the flesh of my hip then up and under my tucked up nightie. His thumb just catches the outer-edge of my breast. The urge that I've held in for so many years has re-awoken and it tears through my body and mind, heating me up in an instant.

Jim's insistent hand moves higher, but is trapped beneath the cotton which has wrapped around me like a cocoon. I pull away from his lips, drag the nightdress up and over my body, and throw it over my shoulder, not caring where it might land. He is sitting up beside me, and as soon as the material has been tossed away his hand is on my breast, cupping it and feeling the flesh overspill his large, hard hands.

"So beautiful." He moans as he brings the other hand to cup the other breast, his face once more dropping to the crook of my neck and kissing across the flesh there that feels tender and stretched, as if I might burst forth from it at any second.

I can't take it anymore so I push against him, his body crumpling back down onto the bed with my own hanging over him. I throw my head back and let my breasts hang over his face. He lifts up his head and dives in like a starving lion. His mouth suckles, bites, and nips at me and I mewl with pleasure. He sucks on a nipple and grips the other strumming it like a musical instrument.

I pull away from his grasp and lower my face to his, craving a kiss, the taste of his lips on mine, the dance of our tongues together. He pulls me closer as our lips meet and I slip down onto one elbow, the other hand skimming over his body and down between his legs to find the hard staff pressing through the material of his boxers.

"I want you," I groan as I squeeze him and take a breath. He moans, answering me emphatically without words. I grasp the top of his underwear and tug down, he lends me a hand, then I push material away from him and my hand once more clasps around him. He's so hot and hard that my pussy contracts in pleasure just from the feel of him in my hand. I want to massage him, I want to stroke him, and I want to feel his come on my hand as he erupts. I want to suck him, I want to lick his tip and swallow his cock until I choke as he spurts down my throat.

My wanton sexuality is released now, from a trickle it turns into a rolling waterfall of lust and passion. All shyness, all hesitancy is forgotten as his hands roam down my body and I grasp him tighter, pulling him closer.

"Not yet," he groans, pulling his pelvis away from my grip, "not yet." He kisses me and his hand slips between my thighs. My grasping hands still beside me as I spread my thighs for him so his fingers can trail through my pooling honey and explore between my lips.

"Oh, yes. I need to taste…" he mumbles, almost incomprehensibly. The bedclothes are thrown away as he rolls over and between my spread thighs. I hold my breath as he moves down till his face is parallel with my wet pussy. He gently pries me apart, my wet lips sticking together as he delicately pulls them open. I feel his breath tickling my clit and I bite my lip in anticipation. His thumbs run down my slick lips and then I feel his lips and his tongue and my mind becomes a mess of arousal. I cannot tell now where his fingers end and his mouth starts, all I am aware of is the ecstasy flowing from his sucking and probing.

I grind my pussy against his face, all inhibitions lost. Suddenly my body is remembering what it has missed out on for so long and is drowning itself in the pleasure of the moment. I come with a moan and a jet of liquid that soaks his face and chin.

"Fuck," he curses, shocking me slightly, "you're amazing."

"No, that's you." I pant, "Oh, Jim, please?"

I can't quite put the words together in a sentence that will make sense. I'm not sure I'm ready to beg him quite yet, but luckily, he knows exactly what I am pleading for.

"Oh, yes, Emily. I'm going to." He pulls up onto his knees and grabs my hips, dragging me down the bed till his cock prods at my wet opening. I wonder at his strength as my breasts and stomach wobble, my cheeks flush and a moment of doubt sets in. It is hard to shrug off the impression that you're too fat to be attractive when it has been the predominant thing taught you by life.

However, Jim doesn't even pause for breath. His cock thrusts into me, slowly at first, then when he feels just how wet and open I am he drives in a little harder. His body arches over me now, his strong arms either side of me, protecting me as his cock ravages me. I am once again overtaken by sheer lust and pleasure as my pussy rediscovers the joy of being full of cock. He stretches me and tickles me in a way that makes me mewl and thrash my head upon the mattress. I reach up and clasp my arms around him, holding tightly to his strong shoulders as he fucks me with such gracious ferocity.

"So good." He groans, speeding up. "So good, oh Emily."

I dig my nails into his shoulders as he roars with his cock pressed deep inside of me, throbbing and pulsing as he fills me with his come. My pussy contracts with pleasure, ripples of orgasms running through me from pelvis to mind and back again, suffusing me with the heat and glow of a good fuck.

"Merry Christmas," he pants, as he collapses beside me.

"Merry Christmas," I reply, laughing. "I'm so glad Santa gave you my present to pass on, though."

He laughs, too, holding me close and kissing my hair.

"Oh, so am I." He grins, and then yawns. "So am I."

* * * *

"Morning, Sunshine." Jim smiles at me as my eyelids flicker open.

"Mmm, hiya." I'm not at my best in the mornings, but I'm slightly disorientated by having a face so close to mine after ten years of waking up alone.

"Are you ready for some breakfast?" he asks, and it's only then I realise he's on top of the blankets and fully dressed.

"How long have you been up for, then?" I ask.

"Oh, an hour or so. I had to get up to sort out the turkey."

"Right, oh yes. Merry Christmas." I smile and he leans in and kisses me.

"And yes, I'd love some breakfast." I'm awake now and hungry. Sex always makes me hungry. I ease my naked self from beneath the covers, the bangs and clangs from the kitchen a comforting sound as I rush over to my clothes and slip on my clean underwear. After slipping into the red dress I pull open the curtains and let the bright winter light stream in.

The street is covered in a fine dusting of frost, like icing sugar on a delicate cake. It's so quiet outside, not a soul wanders along the road. There are no cars, either. Everyone is home enjoying the presents, the food and the love of Christmas, including me this year. I smile and my whole body, mind and soul are in that smile for the first time in many years.

* * * *

"That smells so good, sure you don't need any help in there?"

"No, love, I've got it under control."

I shrug. The scent of turkey, Brussels sprouts, and gravy hangs decadently in the air and the food is overflowing the plate when he brings it over.

"Merry Christmas." He grins as we pull open a cracker.

"Ditto!" I reply as we pull my cracker and I fish out my red Christmas crown and place it on my head. "This is a feast, Jim."

"And there is still a pile left in the kitchen, I'll never eat it all."

"Well, let's take it over to the church then. Doesn't Father Brian welcome in the homeless there today?"

"Oh yes, he does. What a good idea."

We chomp silently, enjoying the succulent turkey and all the trimmings. I especially savour the melt in my mouth, butter-laced mashed potatoes as I've never been able to do them so well myself. As Jim clears away the plates and brings over the Christmas cake I exclaim, "If we pop home I've got a couple of Christmas cake slabs left and we can take those over for Brian, too."

"Great idea," Jim beams, "You're really getting back into the swing of this Christmas thing, aren't you?"

"I am, Jim, thank you so much."

"No need to thank me, it was there all along. I mean, look at this gorgeous Christmas cake, and taste it. You've always had the Christmas spirit, you've just been hiding it of late."

I lean over and kiss him on the forehead. "Sweet man."

"Mmm, sweet cake," he mumbles, biting into his slice. I bite my own and the spice, brandy, and fruit explode on my tongue. Then the blanket of icing and marzipan finish off the mouthful with a sweet, velvety experience that is so evocative of Christmas.

"We best get this over to the Church, love." Jim covers plates and bowls with foil.

"Aye," I stand up and groan, "or I'll never move again, I'm so full."

We laugh and joke all the way to the church, and it is such a wonderful thing to see the gratitude on the faces of Father and the poor homeless and lonely people who have gathered in the church on this holiest of days.

"Well, it looks like they were enjoying that," I comment to Jim as he drives us back to his flat,

"Oh, yes, I'm glad. It's easy to forget about the poor sometimes because you're so absorbed in enjoying your Christmas and buying presents for your loved ones, but it's good to do something. I feel like I've actually helped, actually been a Christian, you know?"

I nod. I do know, but with Jim talking about Christmas presents I realise I've bought him nothing, and suddenly I feel embarrassed. What can I give this man? He's given me so much.

"You've gone quiet," Jim observes as we sit on the sofa. He slips his arm over my shoulders and pulls me close, "Are you okay?"

"I was just thinking," I turn to face him, his arm still around me. "I've not bought you a Christmas present." I see his lips part and I know he's going to hush me, so I slap my finger over his mouth, his gentle lips close as I continue. "So I was wondering what I could give you because you've given me my Christmas back. I've enjoyed this day for the first time in ten years. I've remembered what it's all about and I'd still be playing the miserable old widow if it wasn't for your intervention. So I've thought and thought and I do have something very special that you can have, if you want it."

I take a deep breath and stand up. I lift the hem of my dress and pull it over my head.

"I know, you've already had this," I smile as I shake off my shoes and inch the flesh-coloured tights down my thighs, "and this is not my present."

"Oh, but it was a sweet, sweet present," he groans as I step out of the pantyhose and leave them in a pile on the floor.

"Well, this present is special." I reach behind me and pull open the bra clasp. I pull the straps down my arms and pull the bra away, letting my large globes rest naturally on my chest. I am thrilled to hear him gasp.

"I had to think really hard of a decent present to give you." I take a deep breath and turn round so my back is facing him. I bend over and skim my satin panties down and throw them onto the pile with the other clothing. "So this is my present to you." I run my hands over my buttocks, pulling them apart slightly and displaying to him my wet pussy and the dark, secret hole a little higher.

I straighten up and turn round once more. "I gave my official virginity away many, many years ago, but I still have one cherry to give away, and I want you to have it, well, if you want it, that is."

"Oh, Emily, I want it." He growls, leaping up from the sofa and crushing me to him, his clothed body rubbing my naked flesh so sensually. "I really want it." He pushes his lips to mine and kisses me roughly. I step back and he presses me again, pushing me up against the bedroom door. He continues the passionate kiss as he opens the door and we stumble into the bedroom.

I rip open his shirt, my fingers fumbling over his buttons as he undoes his fly. His jeans fall to the floor. "You're gorgeous," he moans, letting his hands slip up and down my body, caressing my full breasts and pulling them into his hands, "so beautiful."

I fall onto the bed, the springs creaking a little, and we giggle. The room is suffused in a male musk smell—his new aftershave from a distant cousin or someone I can't quite remember, but it's hard to remember anything with Jim nibbling on my breasts, cradling them carefully in his strong hands completely fascinated by them, thank goodness. I had been worried that the sight of my less than perky breasts and my body might turn him off, but he is feasting on me like I'm a Christmas banquet.

"Are you ready for your present?" I groan, eager to get on with it as my stomach is queasy with nervousness.

"Yes." He groans, "Oh, hell yes."

He moves off the bed and I position myself on my hands and knees. I hear him place something on the bedside cabinet, then his strong arms are around me, pushing pillows beneath my tummy to help hold me up.

"What a present." He whistles, skimming his hands over my buttocks and fluttering his fingers between my cheeks, teasing my tight hole and then dipping lower into my honey-soaked pussy. He probes my slit, his fingers sliding inside of me, and I groan, wriggling back to take more of him inside of me.

"Oh, yes," he encourages, slipping his fingers out. I moan and hear a lid being twisted off something, and soon I feel a cold, soft mass pressing between my buttocks. He massages the cold cream onto my tight hole, and his condom-covered cock skims against my thighs as I pant for release.

I gasp as his fingertip enters me, and he strokes my buttock with his other hand as he presses it deeper. I start to clench but then realise that I need to relax, so I take a deep breath and his finger slips in even more, sending sexy shivers though out my body. It feels weird, invasive even, but I'm so turned on by it and the idea of him fucking his cock into this sacred place makes me quake with desire.

"My cock is aching for you." He gasps, and I feel the head pressing against my naturally lubricated opening. He presses forward and soon his cock is embedded in me as well as his finger.

"Oh, so full." I exclaim as he moves back and forward, the sensations radiating from both my holes driving me mad with lust. His finger see-saws in and out of my tight hole easily now and I moan in pure pleasure when I feel another finger entering with it.

"So good," he groans, and he pulls out of my wet pussy. "I gotta move on baby, or I'll fill you there."

His fingers leave me too and I mewl discontent to have two gaping holes and nothing to fill them. He so gently presses his cock into my tight hole and I gasp as the head pops in.

"Stroke your clit," he commands. "It'll feel so good."

So I reach a hand round, letting my body weight rest on the pillows beneath me. I cup my pubis, slipping a finger down through my tight curls into the slickness of my slit, catching the tip of my erect clit.

"That's it." He hisses and slips his cock in further as I moan. I bite back the panic as this strange fullness hits me, it's almost painful. Yet, as I keep swirling my finger in lazy circles over my clit, the pain turns to erotic pleasure.

"Almost there," he pants. I know he's holding back. I can hear the grit in his voice and I appreciate his gallantry.

"Oh yes, fuck me," I shout out, the raw dirtiness of this act taking over me.

"Oh, yeah. Yeah, I'm gonna fuck this arse, baby." He pulls back, then pushes in quicker than before, building up a rhythm.

The pressure is completely different, I feel so full and it is almost too much, but I keep up the teasing of my clit, and the contrast between the two sexy feelings sets my body on fire. I groan, pant, and hiss—words fall from my lips but I don't even comprehend them. I am on a one-way slide, twirling and curling on my way down to the big orgasmic splash and into a pool of ecstasy.

"Can't take it any more," he exclaims.

"Fill me. Fill me!" I demand as my orgasm breaks, my whole body shaking and contracting as the pleasure overwhelms me. His cock thickens and he comes with an exclamation.

"Yes!" His cock rams deep into my tight, no longer virgin hole.

I pant as he gently pulls out of me while stroking my body.

"Did you like your present?"

"I loved it," he replies, and I roll over, meeting his gaze. "And I love you, Emily, you know that, don't you?"

"Yes," I smile, beaming with joy. "Oh yes, and I love you too, Jim, so very much."

He rolls onto the bed beside me, clasping me to him, kissing me with a sweet ferocity. My heart thumps with anticipation.

"I don't know how I'm going to better that next Christmas," I chuckle.

He laughs, "Oh, I'm sure you'll think of something, sweetheart. I'm sure you'll think of something."

And I'm pretty sure I will. When you let the joy and gladness of Christmas into your soul inspiration and love surely follow.

* * * *

About the Authors

Sammie Jo Moresca is a proud card carrying member of the Romance Writers of America, dabbling in erotic romance since 2005. She blushes and tells her friends not to buy her steamy books. Sammie Jo married the firefighter who saved her life and they are living their fairy tale happily ever after.

Meg Winston collects speeding tickets, coffee cups, and characters. She's single because none of the men in her life match the men in her head. She's deliriously happy. Don't tell her cat.

Leigh Ellwood writes spicy romances and sassy mysteries. She is the creator of the award-winning Dareville series for Phaze Books, as well as numerous shorts for Phaze and other small publishers. Readers are invited to visit LeighEllwood.com for more information on Leigh's books, and to follow Leigh's writing adventures via her blog at leighwantsfood. blogspot.com or through her Twitter at Twitter.com/ LeighEllwood.

Victoria Blisse is a mother, wife, Christian, Manchester United fan and erotica writer. She is equally at home behind a laptop or a cooker and she loves to create stories, poems, cakes and biscuits that make people happy. She was born near Manchester, England and her northern English quirkiness shows through in all of her stories. Passion, love and laughter fill her works, just as they fill her busy life. If you want to know more about Victoria and her books please check out her website at http://www. victoriablisse.co.uk Victoria loves to make new friends, so if you're on Myspace pop over and say hello: http://www.myspace.com/victoriablisse Or send an e-mail to her at Victoria@victoriablisse.co.uk .

PHAZE SUPPORTS
EROTIC ALTRUISM

TAKE A FEW HOT FANTASIES TO BED

PHAZE Presents ...

Fantasies
volume I

four tales of erotic romance by ...
Alessia Brio
Leigh Ellwood
Bridget Midway
Ann Regentin

Presents ...

ntasies
volume II

of erotic romance by ...
Will Belegon
Petula Caesar
Sarah Dickson
Stella & Audra Price

PHAZE Presents ...

Fantasies
volume III

tales of homoerotic romance by ...
James Buchanan
Jade Falconer
Eliza Gayle
Jamie Hill
Selah March
Yeva Wiest

PHAZE Presents ...

Fantasies
volume IV

four tales of erotic romance by ...
Vivien Dean
Eva Gale
Philippa Grey-Gerou
Cat Johnson

Presents ...

ntasies
volume V

of erotic romance by ...
Victoria Blisse
L.E. Bryce
Kate Burns
Emma Wildes

PHAZE Presents ...

Fantasies
volume VI

tales of erotic romance by ...
Yvette Hines
Augusta Li
Jude Mason
Derek Musgrave
Jessie Verino
and JN